OVERNIGHT WIFE

PENNY WYLDER

Copyright © 2019 Penny Wylder

All rights reserved. Except as permitted under the U.S. Copyright Act of 1976, no part of this publication may be reproduced, distributed, or transmitted in any form or by any means without prior written permission of the author.

This is a work of fiction. Names, places, characters and incidents are either products of the author's imagination or used fictitiously and any resemblance to actual persons, living or dead, or businesses, organizations, or locales, is completely coincidental.

Thanks for Reading!

Sign up for my newsletter and leave your panties at the door!

Sign up HERE!

1

MARA

"To girls' trip!" My best friend Lea laughs and raises her shot glass to clink it against mine.

I take a deep breath, trying not to let the cloying scent of tequila or the stickiness of this nightclub floor get to me. Or the absolutely terrible layout and lighting situation. Did they really think blue underlighting would flatter *anybody*? Amateurs. I knock my shot—calling it a glass feels far too classy for the plastic neon glowing-in-UV-light container— against Lea's and toss it back without breathing again. That helps to dull the immediate throat and nostril burn of the tequila as it slides down my throat.

With a triumphant "Ha!" I slam my second shot down against the countertop. The cheap plastic container promptly breaks in two pieces. I shoot the bartender a wry smile as he reaches over to scoop it up, rolling his eyes.

Lea, on the other hand, elbows me, looking for all her worth like a proud mama bird who's just shoved its poor fledgling out of the nest headfirst. "Look at you! Mara Greene, a regular party girl. Who'd have thought."

I roll my eyes. "This is *not* going to become a trend, Lea."

"Hey, a girl can dream." Her grin widens as she grabs my hand and tugs me toward the dance floor. This particular overly loud beat *does* sound pretty familiar, in a way that reminds me of college, where Lea and I met. She was the loud and bossy socialite majoring in acting, I was the nerdy shy girl on stage crew who preferred to operate the spotlight rather than stand in front of it. Normally you wouldn't peg the two of us as being a good match, but Lea marched right up to me after I worked on a background set for her solo tryout, wrapped me in a hug and announced that anyone as good with staging as I was had to be her friend.

We've been close ever since. Even if we don't share too many weekend activities—Lea's more of the club scene girl, and I'm more of the "in bed by 9pm so I can wake up pre-dawn to go fishing with my father" type.

A pang that has nothing to do with the tequila strikes me right in the chest. Right above my heart. I rub at it, wincing, and try to force my thoughts away from my father. It's been two years since he passed, but it still hurts just as much as it did on the day he died.

"Are you gonna start dancing, or do I need to buy you another tequila?" Lea shouts in my ear over the heavy thud of the bass.

I sway my hips in tune to the music and she flashes me an approving grin. I have to admit, after the tequila works its way into my bloodstream and I start to work up a sweat on the dance floor, it *does* feel nice to cut loose.

"So?" Lea calls again, when that song peters out and before the next one gets up to full speed. "How are you loving Vegas?" Her eyes twinkle with amusement.

I laugh and roll my eyes. She talked me into driving out here from LA where we both moved after graduation last summer. Lea's waitressing and going on auditions every

Overnight Wife 3

spare moment. And me? I just landed my dream job. Like an actual, honest-to-goodness stage coordinator gig, designing and building props for a huge media company, Pitfire Media, hosting their first play at the biggest theater in the city.

So, some celebrations are in order. As well as a much-needed break from reality for Lea.

Hence my agreeing to this madness. "I guess it's not the worst," I shout back at her, even though, to be honest, I'm having a lot more fun than I expected.

"You're gonna be a club regular by the time the weekend's up," Lea promises, and I snort.

"This is a special occasion. Besides, it's your fault. What did you tell me? 'You need to learn how to cut loose'?"

Lea grins. "I stand by that declaration."

"Then you'd better be ready to help with the consequences tomorrow, when I need a metric ton of caffeine and Tylenol just to crawl out of bed."

Lea shoves my shoulder playfully. "Rule number one of Vegas, Mara: we do *not* worry about next-day consequences while we're still out."

With that, she spins away from me to wrap her arms around the neck of the nearest guy. He's pretty cute actually, tall and gangly and not at all Lea's usual burly macho type. But maybe she's trying new things tonight, too.

I wonder if I can be that brave. Before the thought is even in my head, though, I'm dismissing it. I didn't come here to hook up with someone. I just came to celebrate my new job. End of list. But cutting loose is going to be hard to do with my mind still stuck in LA, wondering how my first day on the job will go the day after tomorrow.

Pitfire is a huge deal. They're new, but they're already big in both LA and New York, not to mention a few smaller cities between. They expanded fast, like startup-level fast, thanks to their extremely young CEO. The CEO who everyone tells me is the most eligible bachelor in LA.

Not that I plan on mixing work and pleasure. Tequila might burn, but *that* is a cocktail with disaster written all over it.

My head buzzes pleasantly as I skip back toward the bar after the next song, leaving Lea wrapped up with her new friend, intent on finding some water. This buzz is ideal, but if I dehydrate too much, I don't want to know how bad I'll feel in the morning.

As I walk over, I cast a discerning eye around the club. The lights, if anything, are even worse by the bar than they are in the middle of the room. You'd think that a club with as great a reputation as this one—not to mention one that pulls in so much money—would be able to afford a nicer lighting setup. Or even a stage with any sort of backdrop, instead of just a dingy, stained red curtain to hide the yucky bare black walls.

Oh well. There's no accounting for taste. And while Vegas has been more fun than I expected, classy and tasteful aren't exactly words I'd use to describe it.

"Buy you a drink?" asks a guy near the bar. He grins at me, but his eyes do that long, lingering up-and-down thing that tells me he's already undressing me in his head. Then he actually has the nerve to lick his lips afterward.

"Thanks, but I'm good," I reply before I move to step around him toward a less crowded section of the bar.

That's when he grabs my hand to stop me. I'm staring at him open-mouthed, shocked at the nerve, while he rubs his palm against mine, his eyebrows shooting up with surprise. "You've got a lot of callouses for a pretty young thing." He tugs me toward him and I try to wrench myself free, waking

Overnight Wife   5

from my stupor at last. But his grip is too tight. He's got corded muscles visible all up both arms. Bigger muscles than I have, despite my day job doing heavy lifting and construction work, and I'm no match for him.

"There's no shame in hard work," I tell him, narrowing my eyes. With one last tug, I wrench my hand free. He staggers a step, but rights himself before I can make a break for it.

"What kinda hard work do you do?" He gives me the once-over again—or I guess the twice-over now—and my stomach churns with nausea.

"The kind that's none of your business," I snap, already turning on my heel to leave. I storm off the dance floor, away from the bar. There's a little corner a few steps away that looks fairly abandoned. Yes, okay, hiding in a darkened corner wouldn't exactly earn Lea's approval, but I need a break from this party girl lifestyle. Clearly it is not my thing.

I lean against the wall and let my head fall back against it, my eyes drifting shut. I can feel the thump of the bass through the wall I'm leaning against and through the soles of my feet. I smell the sticky scent of sweat and spilled rum and cokes, too. But at least I've got a little bit of breathing room now. Enough to clear my head and get the sensation of that creepy guy's touch off my body.

Just then, I sense warmth at my arm. I crack one eyelid to spot someone approaching my hiding spot, and I stiffen, expecting that guy to try again. Guys like that don't know when to quit.

But the man who stops in front of my hidey-hole is unfamiliar. I tilt my head back to squint up at him. He's tall and dressed more like he's about to walk into a board room than into a club. He's unbuttoned his dress shirt cuffs and rolled them up far enough to give me a glimpse of his strong, veined forearms. His tie is loose around his neck. His dark eyes dance with amusement when they catch mine.

"Don't worry," he says, his voice low and yet still audible over the blast of the music, a trick I wish I could steal for when I'm on set and shouting into my mic to be heard over rehearsal music. "Your new friend won't be bothering you anymore."

I glance past this guy toward the doors and I spot two bouncers escorting the creep out of the club, while he tries to twist out of their arms, protesting. It brings a small smile to my face. "Your doing?" I ask.

"I don't like men who can't take no for an answer," he replies. "Especially not ones who insult the concept of hard work while they're at it."

My cheeks flush, and I hope this guy can't see it in the dark of the club. "Well, thanks for that, knight in...slightly disheveled suit." I gesture at him with a grin.

He returns it, and oh, damn. He is even hotter than I thought at first. The club lights illuminate sharp hollows under his cheekbones and a sturdy brow. He's got the kind of face that makes you immediately think about how he'd be in bed: stern and commanding, a total dom in the best possible way. "I agree with you, you know," he says. "About hard work. There's no shame in it."

He takes a step closer, and I couldn't back away if I wanted to, with the wall at my back, and me still leaning against it. Besides, I don't want to. I raise my chin to keep my eyes locked on his, even though he's a good head taller than me. "That why you look like you just stepped out of a board room, even though you're in the middle of a club in Vegas?" I ask, surprising myself with my audacity. Normally I don't really talk to guys. I don't bother. I'm too busy for a relationship.

Overnight Wife

7

But this could never be a relationship. Hook ups in Vegas don't become anything more than just that. And maybe a hook up is what I need. After all, I've been working my ass off at school for years. When I finally graduated, I worked my ass off some more at internships and applying for jobs, until I finally landed my dream gig. This is my one weekend to let off steam before I have to become a responsible adult. Before I start working full-time, and God knows how long it'll be before I have the chance to do anything even remotely resembling a casual hook up again.

My mystery man laughs, like he's startled, too. Good. Something about his serious demeanor makes me want to surprise him. To catch him off his guard and make him laugh, if I can. "What can I say? The club scene isn't normally my beat. Wound up here by chance." He's grinning as he says it, his gaze sweeping over me. But unlike the creeper, it doesn't bother me when this guy checks me out.

In fact, I'd like him to keep doing it. If nothing else, it will distract him from noticing that I'm doing the same thing to him. Giving that sexy body of his a once over of my own, because damn, that suit fits him perfectly. And it makes me wonder how it would look on my hotel room floor.

"What a coincidence," I call back to him, raising my voice as the music gets louder. "Me too."

"Well, we should celebrate then. What are you drinking?" He winks at me and holds out an arm, like a real gentleman. Right here in the middle of a bunch of gyrating clubgoers, it strikes me as even more unusual.

I loop my arm through his. "Tequila, mostly," I admit, and I'm gratified to see him cringe.

"You need something more suitable. What do you usually drink, when you're not clubbing in Vegas?"

I laugh. "I don't know. I'm not much of a drinker. Something simple, maybe. Not too sweet." He leans across the bar and orders us both vodka tonics—top shelf, I notice. "You don't have to do that," I call in his ear. "I'm fine with well drinks."

"You shouldn't be," he replies, amusement dancing in his dark eyes. "A girl like you deserves top shelf everything."

For some reason, those words send a curl of pleasure through my belly. Even more so when he trails a hand up my arm to rest on my shoulder, his fingertips alighting so gently on my skin that they raise goosebumps the whole way up. I shiver, unable to suppress it, and his grin widens, as if he knows exactly what he's doing to me.

He probably does. Bastard.

It makes me want more.

The bartender passes us our drinks—it didn't take long at all, not like when Lea and I ordered shots before. I suspect the bartender must have been keeping an eye out for this guy. Probably because he's the type to buy top shelf liquor in a club like this.

"What's your name?" I call into his ear. Unless I'm mistaken, he flinches for a second, as though hesitating.

"John," he calls back. Okay. No last names. I can dig it. We are, after all, in Vegas. The land of anonymity. That's fair enough.

"I'm Mara." I stick out my hand, which seems hilariously formal and awkward after I do it, making another blush bloom across my cheeks. But John just places my drink into my hand and leans in until his lips graze my ear.

"It's a pleasure to meet you, Mara."

I swear, if a guy could make you come with his voice alone, John is the one who would do it. Deep and baritone, it vibrates all the way through my body, making my thighs

Overnight Wife 9

tighten and my belly clench. I shift a little closer to him as I take my a sip of my drink.

Wow. I never really thought of well drinks as that much different from the better versions, but after a night of crappy tequila and mixed vodka drinks, the difference is stark, even to my already-tipsy senses. This tastes miles better than any vodka cran or vodka and lime drink I concocted back in my dorm room with the cheapy bottles I could afford back then

.

I raise my glass to toast John, and as they clink together, I grin at him. "So. Two hardworking non-partiers meet at a club... that sounds like the start of a joke."

"Or the start of a very promising evening," he murmurs, which makes me inhale, tense again, for all the right reasons.

Without waiting for me to finish the drink, John takes my free hand and leads me toward the dance floor. "I thought you didn't club," I call to him.

He smirks. "No. But that doesn't mean I can't dance." With that, he shifts his arm to my waist, pinning me against him. I drape my arms around his shoulders, my drink still in hand, the cool glass pressed against his back. He does the same, and his cold glass chills the nape of my neck, making me shiver again—but also offering a welcome respite from the heat beginning to build in this club tonight.

I lean in close to him, and he shifts his hips against mine. I follow his rhythm, swaying with him. He wasn't wrong. He's a good dancer, which for some reason surprises me. But I follow, and he holds me closer, and I try to ignore the way I can feel him growing hard, his erection stiffening through the tight fabric of his pants. His cock is pressed right against my belly, digging into me hard enough that I can practically measure the length.

Huge.

I sway with him, and neither of us says a word about how aroused we're getting, even though I know if I checked my panties right now, they'd already be soaked, and he's barely even touched me.

John spins me around so my back is to him, and I move against him, getting into the rhythm. I take another sip from my vodka, and glance out across the floor, catching Lea's eye. She flashes me a thumbs-up and raises an eyebrow, the universal girl code for "you all good?" I flash one back and grin so she knows my dance is 100% consensual and much enjoyed.

She winks and goes back to her own partner, the same cute guy I noticed her dancing with earlier.

The song fades and another one starts. Next thing I know, I've finished my drink. I lean back against him, going up on tiptoes to shout in his ear. "Another one?" I ask.

"Are you sure?" His gaze dances over to me, more amused than anything else. "You seem a little loose on your feet already."

I narrow my eyes. "I am a grown woman, thank you very much. And I would like more of that delicious top shelf vodka of yours. Unless you're going to make me go back to well..."

He laughs and catches my hand, pulling it to his lips. He kisses the back of my knuckles, then leans down to kiss my jawline, just below my ear. "I wouldn't dare," he whispers, his breath hot on my skin, tickling all over.

Then he weaves back through the club toward the bar, and right around there is where my night grows fuzzy...

* * *

Overnight Wife

There were other clubs. I remember that much. There's a flash of a pub, with Lea and her boy in tow. Another club, this one with flashing strobe lights. I remember dancing with John again, his lips meeting mine for the first time, hard and insistent. He tasted just like the top shelf vodka—like the kind of quality kiss I'd never tasted before.

And he's so damn hot.

There was more, I know that. Some kind of red room, lined in silk... a lot of cheering, balloons maybe? Or confetti? I don't know. The next thing I remember is stumbling up to John's room, by coincidence in the same hotel where Lea and I were staying, albeit definitely not on the budget floor where we booked. When he opens the door, I actually gasp aloud.

The penthouse is huge. There's a jacuzzi in it, and a living room and kitchen connected to an even larger bedroom, with a comically huge bed. I barely have time to take it all in before John kisses me, and this time he doesn't let up. I wrap my arms around his neck and arch up into him, my hips digging into him the way they did earlier when we danced.

His lips part mine, his tongue slips between my lips, and I lose myself in his taste, the feel of his hands gripping my hips, pulling me closer to him.

He hoists me up, and I wrap my legs around his waist, my pussy pressed right against his belt buckle, so I can feel the size of his hard cock as he walks me toward the bedroom. With every step, I can feel myself shifting against him, getting wetter, hotter, as he deepens the kiss.

A little voice in my head wants to second guess this. But it's been so long since I hooked up with anyone, so long since I let loose and had some fun. This is Vegas, after all. This is what you're supposed to do. So even though part of me wonders if I should be doing this, a bigger part yells shut up.

After all, tomorrow starts a new phase in my life. Tomorrow, my world is going to change. So tonight, I'm allowed to have a little fun, dammit.

At least, that's what I tell myself. But it gets easier to stop worrying when John drops me on the bed, and pins me in place with one arm, kissing me again before he leans back to spear me with a heated glance. "Spread your legs," he orders, and the man does not have to tell me twice.

I spread my legs as wide as they'll go, and shiver with anticipation as he kneels at the edge of the bed and peels my panties off. When his hot lips touch the inside of my thigh and he starts to kiss his way up the sensitive skin, there's not a shred of doubt left in my body.

I can let myself have this one night of fun. Tomorrow, everything will be different.

2

MARA

I groan. My mouth feels like there's a gasoline soaked rag stuffed inside, and behind my eyes, there's a headache throbbing in full force. I reach up to fling an arm across my forehead, but the movement only makes the throbbing worse. Not to mention, the motion sends a wave of nausea through my body, and my stomach clenches, roiling from the simple movement. "Dear God, why," I groan, forgetting where I am. Wanting nothing more than to make the aching stop.

"Take this," murmurs an unfamiliar voice. One that immediately makes me slide my arm up off my eyes and crack my eyelids with worry.

Oh. Right. I forgot about *him*.

John sits on the edge of the bed, a knowing smirk on his face as he presses a glass of water and a couple of pills into my palm. I squint at them suspiciously until he chuckles. "Relax. It's just Advil."

I decide if he was going to drug me... well, he probably would've done that last night. Not that he needed to—I was all about the hookup. Flashes of it come back to me, and my cheeks burn from the memories. I have a fuzzy memory of riding him, my bra still on, screaming his name as he urged me to ride his fat cock, I believe were the words.

Blushing, I stuff the pills into my mouth and swallow them with several gulps of water. On second thought, I wind up draining the entire glass. Better safe than sorry.

Then I pass it back to him, wincing as another onslaught of memories reminds me how I knelt in front of him on all fours begging for his cock in my mouth. Or how he spanked me when he was fucking me from behind...

Damn. I've always had a lot of kinky fantasies, but I've never felt comfortable enough to actually act them out with anybody. Maybe because I'd never met John before and I knew nothing serious would ever come of our hookup—not to mention the fact that I'll never see him again after today —I was able to let go and be less inhibited.

Either way, it was a damn good night, I know that much. But it's also, in retrospect, very embarrassing. I can't wait to slip out of here and find Lea, join her for coffee and swap conquest stories over brunch.

"Well, thanks for the painkillers, clearly needed, but I'll —" I stop talking, realizing John has wandered off. Oh well. Probably for the best. I glance past the bed at the bathroom door, and the one look reminds me all over again how fancy this room is. What does this guy do? Maybe he's got a trust fund or something. He's older than me, that much is clear, but not by a lot. It's hard to imagine a guy his age having enough money to throw around that he can afford a swanky penthouse in one of the most expensive hotels on the strip. Then again, I'm not about to complain. This will probably be the only time I'll ever see the inside of a suite like this.

I slip out of bed and pad toward the bathroom. Inside, I rub sleep from my eyes and squint blearily at my surround-

Overnight Wife 15

ings. I have to check twice, just to make sure I'm not imagining it. Nope. Full bathtub with jacuzzi jets, an enormous rain shower that could accommodate a small family... complete with a one-way mirror looking out over Vegas. We're at the top of one of the tallest buildings in the city. The view is breathtaking.

I turn on the shower and rinse myself off, all while gaping at that view. It's almost enough to distract me from my memories of last night.

Almost, but not quite.

But there's one memory in particular bugging me. The red room with Lea in tow...

I'm still thinking about that when my hand catches in my hair. I curse under my breath and struggle to disentangle it. Then I frown at my fingers. There's a big diamond—gotta be fake—on my left hand. It sparkles when I move it, catching the light, almost like a real one... Impressive.

But why am I wearing it?

Shaking my head, I finish toweling off and check my phone. Several dozen missed texts from Lea.

Photos, I realize. I open them and click through. And with every successive photo, my stomach sinks lower, my jaw dropping, my knees going weak.

No. Oh, fuck no. We didn't.

But there it is, right in photographic evidence. A series of pictures of me and John, in a red-painted chapel with Elvis serving as the officiant and... marrying us! There are processional pictures, too. Lea giving me away, some selfies of Lea and the guy she took out last night. And then a series of shots of me and John. Holding hands, kissing... then me leaping up to wrap my legs around his waist and seriously make out.

At that point it goes back to selfies of Lea giving me a thumbs-up. She labeled that one "YOU GO GIRL."

I cannot fucking believe this.

I stumble back into the bedroom, forgetting I'm only wearing a towel.

"There you are." John catches my eye with a grin. He's carrying a tray in his arms. Breakfast, I realize. He must have ordered room service for us. I can smell bacon and eggs from here, and my stomach growls with desire.

But...

"Did we get *married* last night?" I blurt, unable to stop myself.

He goes quiet, his expression suddenly serious.

I hold up my hand accusingly, diamond facing out. "I woke up and found this on my finger. And... and... I've got all these pictures that Lea just sent me, of us in a chapel with an Elvis impersonator. I mean... fuck! Is this real?"

"What do you think?" he asks softly.

"I fucking hope it's not!" I yell, flinging my arms wide. "I can't *get married*, least of all to some rando I met in a club in Las Vegas for God's sake."

His expression shifts into a scowl. "Is there something wrong with me?" He arches one eyebrow. "You didn't seem to think so last night when you were begging for my cock."

My cheeks flare red hot. "I didn't—I mean..." I groan. "That's not what I meant, and you know it. Last night was fun." I pause. Blush again. "*Really* fucking fun."

His smirk widens, and he glances down at my towel, setting the breakfast tray aside. "Then why don't you drop the towel and we can continue the fun. I seem to remember something about you wanting me to fuck you in the shower, although it seems you beat me there this morning..."

My breath hitches. Tempting. Oh, how fucking tempt-

Overnight Wife   17

ing. But my head is still throbbing, and this conversation is hardly helping. "That's not important right now," I mutter. "What's important is *fixing this*. How do we…" I can't even believe I'm about to say these words. "How do we annul our marriage? Get it invalidated or whatever."

His expression darkens. "Oh trust me, that part is easy."

Something about the look makes my curiosity flicker. Has he done this before? But he steps toward me, distracting me from any thoughts about his past.

"Why are you in such a rush, Mara? I didn't think you'd be upset about this." His expression turns mischievous. "Pretty sure you weren't upset last night. How many times did you come? I lost count at ten."

My face could light this whole suite on fire right now. But I ball up my fists, trying to ignore it. The feeling of my nails digging into my palms helps distract me. "I don't understand how you *aren't* upset, John. You don't think this is a complete disaster?"

"Far from it. That was the best sex I've ever had in my life. And I don't think I'm being egotistical when I say it was yours, too."

I hate that I can't disagree. Even with blank spots in my memory, blocking out some of what we did, the parts I *can* remember? Well, let's just say that last night alone could keep me fueled with enough dirty memories to power my fantasies for months.

But still. Hot sex with a stranger in Vegas is one thing. *Marrying* said hot stranger is quite another. "Look, I'm not saying I didn't have fun."

"Then what's the problem?" He arches an eyebrow, and it's so infuriating it makes me want to shake him. Or kiss him. Or let him kiss me, the way he did last night, his tongue tracing a line down my jawline, along the curve of my neck, over my collarbone, until he wound up taking my bra off with his teeth alone.

A feat in and of itself, I can tell you.

My breath hitches. "The *problem* is that we can't stay married, obviously."

That infuriating eyebrow remains arched, as if he disagrees. Yet all he says is, "You want to get this annulled."

"I want my life go to back to normal."

"Normal and lacking in mind-blowing orgasms that make you scream my name so loud we get noise complaints from neighboring rooms?" He's grinning again, and goddamn it, I hate the way he can get to me so easily. We've only known each other for a day. It's not fair that he already knows exactly which buttons to push.

He takes a step toward me, then another. I'm painfully, heatedly aware that I'm still only wearing a towel. My face feels so hot I'm surprised he can't feel the heat radiating off me—and that's nothing compared to the rest of me. My pussy pulses between my thighs, my clit feels swollen with desire. Even if there are parts of last night that I don't recall, I have a feeling my body remembers every single second.

And it wants more.

"What's the hurry, Mara?" John murmurs, and that voice is like silk between my thighs, caressing all the right spots. "We've got all the time in the world. Just take off that towel, come back to bed..."

I set my jaw hard, not sure whether I'm angrier with myself or him right now. "Stop it. I need to think, and I can't with you distracting me. Get out!"

His smirk widens. "You realize you're in *my* room, right?"

With a groan, I grab for my clothes, strewn across the floor in a way that sends a flash of memories rushing

Overnight Wife   19

through my mind. My shirt flying in one direction. My panties very carefully being peeled off in another…

"Breakfast," he says, and for a second, I pause in the middle of collecting my things, positive he's about to hit on me again. But he's smiling, looking actually innocent for once. "I know a great little spot on the corner. Marcelle's. They have a great fire-roasted tomato omelet, good coffee. Let's meet there in an hour, okay? And then we can talk about all of this."

"No, that's not okay," I snap. "Can't we just annul this remotely or something? I have things to do." A job to start tomorrow. The very thought of it almost starts a fresh wave of panic in my body, but I push it away, repress it for now. First things first: get out of this guy's room.

This guy with the alluring eyes and the devilish smile, who's currently looking at me like he wants to devour me whole. This guy who blew my mind last night—and also makes me want to punch him this morning.

This guy who already knows something about annulments, to judge by his reaction every time I bring it up. It makes me wonder whether this is the first time he's done something wild like this, running off and getting married to a stranger. For some insane reason, it makes me jealous to think about him with another woman, doing the things we did. Even though I know that's crazy. I have no claim on him, and he has no claim on me. I don't even *want* to be married to him. So why should it bug me that I'm probably not his first wife?

I shake my head as I head for the door. *Wife.* I'm nobody's wife. That's crazy talk.

"Is that a yes?" John calls after me, and I wave a hand back at him.

"No, it is not," I snap over my shoulder.

"You know, I don't remember you being this stubborn last night when you were begging for my cock," he calls, loud enough that it makes me tense, wondering if anyone can hear—how thin are these walls if we got noise complaints last night?

Or how loud was I being, exactly? The latter seems more likely, and it makes me blush and makes me hot all over again to think about.

Maybe Lea is right. Maybe I should let loose a little more often.

But no. What am I saying? Look at how *this* turned out. With a ring on my finger and a wedding contract I need to wriggle out of.

It doesn't help that my headache and the fog of my hangover have redoubled, making every step I take feel like a mountain to my tired limbs. "Fuck off," I mumble over my shoulder, which just makes John laugh, the bastard. Then I manage to reach the elevator—the elevator that just opens straight up into his suite, damn, how rich *is* this guy? —and hit the button for my floor. I refuse to turn around, even when he calls after me.

"I'll wait for you, darling," he yells, teasing, I think. Probably.

My back tenses. "Don't make me get a restraining order on you."

"Be tricky to sign our annulment papers if you do that, won't it?" he yells back.

It's childish, I know, but the only reply I can think of is to offer him my middle fingers, just as the doors to the elevator slide shut. But that's as much energy as I'm willing to expend fighting him any more on this right now. Because my head has started to pulse and I swear I'm going to be sick if I worry about anything one minute longer.

Overnight Wife   21

I reach my floor and stumble down the hall to my room, swiping the key and making it all the way inside before I remember that I'm sharing this room. And shockingly, in a move that feels patently unfair, Lea is sitting up in her bed already, on the other side of our double room, watching television with a spread of room service around her on the mattress.

She takes one look at me and smirks. "So, I see your wedding night went well."

3

MARA

I slam the door behind me and flop face-first onto my bed with an angry groan that turns into a scream halfway down. "I can't believe you let me do that," I yell when I'm finally ready to turn back over again and glare at my ceiling. "What happened to sisters before misters and all that?"

"Hey, you seemed entirely into it. I mean, the number of times you swore to me you wanted this, honestly—"

"I was drunk!" I wail. "Why didn't you stop me? You know I'm a lightweight."

"Relax, Mara. This kind of thing happens all the time." Lea smiles over at me. "You guys can just go say it was a goofy one-night mistake and get it all cleared up by morning."

"It *is* morning," I point out testily, with a glare at the curtains, as if the bright desert sunlight out there is personally responsible for the terrible decisions I made under the influence last night.

"By tomorrow morning, then." She waves a hand, but the words send a stone ricocheting through my gut.

Tomorrow morning. When I'm supposed to be back in Los

Angeles, ready to start my brand-new dream job at Pitfire Media. I cannot have this hanging over my head while I'm there. It will ruin any chance I have at concentrating on what I'm supposed to be doing. "That's not going to work," I groan. "I need to fix this today, Lea. Tomorrow I won't have time; I need to have my head in the game. This is the worst possible moment for me to decide to go off the rails—"

"Which is probably why your subconscious decided to go wild," she points out. "The harder you suppress your wild side, Mara, the crazier it becomes when it bursts free. Trust me on this one. I've learned it the hard way."

"Yeah? Did *you* get married to a complete stranger yesterday?"

"Well, no..." She smirks. "You might beat me on the wild side front now, actually."

I groan again and grab one of my pillows to bury my face in.

"Come on." Lea pats the bed next to her. "Come over here and have some breakfast. You'll feel better with some food in you."

The word breakfast just reminds me of John. Probably waiting downstairs at that café he suggested, feeling all smug in his knowledge that I'm thinking about him. He thinks I'm just going to cave and come running after him like a good little wife? Well, he's got another thing coming.

I grab the ring, giving it a tug. But it's stuck on my finger, probably because my hands are swollen from the heat and all the booze last night. Nobody warned me how sweaty and yucky hangovers would feel. I can't decide if I want a cold shower or to drink a gallon of water or maybe just fall into a hot tub and drown myself.

"Whoa. I didn't notice *that* last night." Lea crawls over to my bed, and offers me a plate entirely consisting of bacon

Overnight Wife   25

and eggs. I dig into the bacon, unable to stomach the site of the slightly congealing eggs, and crunch on it while she forcibly examines the diamond. "Is that *real*? Holy shit, girl. Maybe you should stay married to this guy. Who the hell did you say he was again?"

I groan. "No idea. John somebody?" I don't even know my husband's last name. What a mess.

"It's probably on your marriage certificate," Lea points out with a sly grin, and I want to smack her all over again. I kick her away with a grumble of annoyance, though not before stealing one last slice of her bacon first.

"It's got to be fake," I say. "He probably bought it at one of the zillion arcade-looking stores on the main street."

"That thing is not plastic," Lea disagrees, but I just stare at the ring, too stubborn to think about what it means if she's right.

"Can we just not talk about it for a while?" I ask. "I'll already have to start researching annulment procedures when we get home. I'd rather not ruin my *whole* day dwelling in the meantime. Especially when we need to get moving."

Lea sighs. "Fun time is over, huh?"

I grimace at the clock next to my bed, all too aware that checkout is in less than an hour. After that, I'll have to drive home, get cleaned up, and figure out how to start the rest of my life tomorrow. "I'm afraid so," I mumble. "Time for the hard work to start."

* * *

Monday morning rolls around all too soon. If I'm honest, I still feel a little fuzzy around the edges, but at least the blinding pain of the hangover has mostly faded, replaced by

a vague gnawing hunger and even more nerves that I antici-
pated for my first day—which is saying something, since I
already expected to be a mess of anxiety from the minute I
walked through the studio doors.

Not to mention, I still can't get this damn ring off. I tried
everything. Coconut oil, running cold water over it... Nothing. It must be way too small for me. But it feels all right on
my finger. It's only when I try to tug it off that my finger
swells up angrily and seems like it's holding onto the damn
thing to spite me.

Great. I can't wait to try and explain that away to my new
coworkers. "Oh, this? Just a joke ring from my not-husband,
haha, yes..."

At least I found out how to annul this damn marriage. It
didn't take long last night, just a few google searches. The
process is simple, but it does require both of our signatures.
Which leaves me with my latest problem, one that only hit
me, helpfully, in the car on my way in to my first day of
work.

I have no way to contact my new husband. In fact, the
only thing I really know about him is that he's probably
wealthy and his name is John. Not exactly a lot to go by. You
can't really search "rich John in Vegas"—believe me, I tried.
The results are... not what you'd expect. Definitely not men
like the one I slept with.

I hope, anyway.

But when I park out front of the theater and glance up at
the big Pitfire Media sign out front, it feels like a weight is
lifting off my shoulders, despite all my first-day jittery
nerves. Because what matters is still on track. My career is in
the right spot. This whole marriage thing is a blip, and a
frustrating one, but I'll solve it.

I'll figure things out, and as long as after it's done I never

Overnight Wife 27

have to deal with my frustrating as hell one night stand again, I'll be golden.

Yes, okay, so he was hot. And sexy. And he's right, he did make me come more than I'd even realized was possible in a single night. And maybe I had a sexy dream about him last night, one that I couldn't even tell if it was a hot memory or a creation of my dirty mind.

In it, he had me pinned across the bed, my hands above my head and clasped in his, while he teased me with his hand between my legs, toying with me right up to the edge of an orgasm, and then stopping, until I was bucking against the sheets, begging for his cock. When he finally slid into me, stretching my walls, stuffing me full of his fat cock, it was everything I'd begged for and more.

But I'm not ready to be a wife. Not to anybody, least of all to a cocksure asshole like him.

Right now, I am all about work. Work first, and everything else second.

That's what I'm reciting in my head as I stride into the general meeting for new hires and find my seat at the back of the room, between a couple other interns who both flash smiles at me. I'm still reciting it as I take out my planner and organize myself on the table, ready to take notes.

But then the doors open, and he walks in.

And my stomach plummets all the way through the concrete floor of this bunkerlike office. Suddenly, I can't breathe. I can't focus on anything, least of all the carefully detailed notes I'd planned on taking.

Because there he is. My new boss, the CEO of Pitfire Media and head of the company I've wanted to work for ever since I moved to Los Angeles.

My new husband, John Walloway, I realize with a sinking sensation in the pit of my stomach. Youngest CEO of a major media company ever, a veritable genius and a workaholic to judge by the tabloid reports—or lack thereof —about him. But he certainly didn't seem work-focused last weekend when he was fucking me six ways from Sunday.

He's glancing around the room, a polite but disinterested smile on his face as he nods to each new hire in turn. Until he reaches me. Then he stops, stutters. It's just for a second, but it's a long enough pause to let me know that he sees me. He realizes what it means that I'm here.

And I'm gratified to realize that he didn't expect this either, at least. He seems just as stunned as I am.

But it doesn't stop the slow, self-satisfied grin that spreads across his face as he keeps his gaze locked onto mine. The sea of people around us seems to vanish, and for a split second, it's just the two of us in this room. He looks like he's just won a damn medal. Like his whole body is bursting with the need to tell me *I knew you couldn't stay away.*

And the worst part is, as I watch him now, I'm afraid he's right.

How the hell am I going to stay away from him now?

4

JOHN

The moment I walk into the conference room on Monday morning, it's like I can sense her. Like the rest of the room fades away and all I can focus on is Mara.

My new wife.

But why is she *here*, of all places? Sitting in the orientation session for Pitfire's newest hires. I don't remember hiring anyone named Mara Greene—I kept our marriage certificate close, so I'd be able to look her up and reach out to her if she stood me up for breakfast yesterday. Which she did. A predictable move.

This, on the other hand... This, I didn't see coming. Which is probably why it makes me grin so much.

That, and it's just a natural reaction to the sensation of my cock stiffening at the sight of her. It's not my fault. One glimpse and I'm back in that hotel room, watching her on all fours in front of me, begging me to put my cock in her mouth, to fuck her from behind on the shag carpet, to spread-eagle her across the bed and have my way with her.

And oh, how I did. Every way I could think of, and yet here I am, still craving more. There aren't many—no, correction, there are *no* women who have done this to me before. Not even my most recent ex, who I'd thought at the time was pretty decent in the sack.

She was nothing compared to Mara. Nobody has been. Which was why I was feeling pretty damn lucky that she's the one who wound up with my mother's vintage ring on her finger. I carry it for sentimental reasons mostly, after my mother foisted it on me years ago, insisting that I find someone to marry and carry on the family name. I'd only really considered putting it on someone's finger once, and every tabloid in America has reported on how well that idea turned out.

But Mara was different. With Mara, after one night I wanted to give her the world.

Then the next morning, she woke up a different person. Acting like I was dirt, some random nobody who tricked her into a marriage she didn't want. As if it hadn't been her idea in the first place.

But something about that reaction, her anger and even her annoyance that I wouldn't just end the marriage after a single night, made me even more certain that I wanted her. Because it told me she wasn't faking. Mara Greene had no idea who I was.

It's written all over her face now too, as she watches me, stunned in shock. She didn't know I was the CEO of the company she'd just joined. She didn't know I'm worth billions. It's not only refreshing, it's reassuring, too. Because she couldn't be a gold-digger, coming after me for my money, trying to drain away my hard-earned work, if she didn't even know I *had* any money.

Well. The ring was probably a clue that I had *some,* but still.

One glance down, and my grin widens. Mara realizes

Overnight Wife   31

her mistake and jerks her hand off the table a second later, flipping the diamond around under her palm, but it's too late. I saw it.

She's still wearing the ring.

That has to mean something, doesn't it?

And now, as much as she hates me—as much as she clearly wanted nothing more to do with me after our night together—here she is. Forced to work under me. I already know from what I got to know of her last weekend that work for Mara is everything: it's her first and last priority, and all the rest in between. She won't quit this job. She'd see it as a point of pride to stick it out.

Which means I've got her at my whim. My smile turns possessive, eager.

Oh, I'll have fun with this. I'll make her wait until she's the one begging me again. Just remembering the sound of her voice as she pleaded with me to let her come again is enough to make my cock inch toward dangerously hard while I'm standing at the front of a room full of employees.

With effort, I tear my gaze from Mara, pleased in the knowledge that I'll have all the time in the world to win her over. And oh, how I intend to. Because she might have fuzzy memories of our wedding night, but I remember every single second. And I'm not about to let her slip through my fingers.

Just wait, little kitten, I think with a smile as I clap my hands for attention to get this meeting started. *Just wait.*

Her eyes lock on mine again, and I could almost swear she's thinking similar thoughts based on the way her eyes widen and her lips part, her cheeks flush in that pink-tinged way they do whenever she's nervous—or hot and eager for action. So probably a little bit of both right now.

"Thank you all for being here today," I say with a broad

smile. "If you've made it this far, then congratulations. You are the cream of the crop. Some of the best this industry has to offer—I should know, because I personally made sure our hiring process is the most rigorous out there." It seems Mara's talk about working hard and playing hard in the club was spot-on, if she's here today. It still surprises me that I didn't recognize her name from the applicant pool while we were dancing—normally I approve every new hire, but last week I was distracted, eager for the weekend and some release. And then when I met her, well... for once in a very, very long time, work was the last thing on my mind.

But it reassures me that we have more in common than she thinks we do, if she's here at Pitfire. She must be determined and smart to have landed this position.

Determined, smart, hot, sexy as hell in bed... I sure chose my new wife well, didn't I?

I force thoughts of her from my mind again while I focus on the new hires, all watching me with upturned faces and eager eyes. "I won't bore you with any long lectures today, as I know you're all eager to get started at your new positions. Your direct managers will explain your day-to-day schedule with you after this meeting, as well as orienting you and training you for any equipment and procedures you may need to learn. I just wanted to call you all in this morning to meet you each individually, face-to-face. As CEO, it can be easy to lose track of people, especially in a company this large."

I look at Mara again, grinning. "So I make it a personal point of pride to get to know each and every one of my employees, from the top all the way on down to our newest hires. If you ever run up against anything you need help with, or any areas where you think the company can improve, my office is always open. I started this company

Overnight Wife　　　　33

from nothing, with nothing but my own ingenuity and creativity. So I always welcome new suggestions, no matter whether they're from long-standing employees or new ones. All of your opinions and ideas matter here at Pitfire."

The room bursts into applause, and I chuckle under my breath. Mara doesn't clap, I notice. She has her hands tightly clasped together under the table, her right hand wrapped protectively around the left one, almost like she's toying with the ring right now. Probably wondering what my game is.

Oh, she has no idea.

I make my way around the room slowly, introducing myself, as promised, to each new hire in turn. I start at the front, and as I go, after a short chat, I dismiss each person to their new gig individually.

Naturally, I save the best for last.

I take my time talking to Tyrone, our newest development lead. He has a lot on his plate, fixing up the websites for some of our media clients. We do have a lot to discuss, but I also draw out our conversation, enjoying the tension on Mara's face. She's the last employee left to talk to.

When Tyrone and I shake hands and say goodbye, I step over to Mara. I wait, in silence, smiling down at her, enjoying the even brighter red flush on her cheeks, until the door of the office clicks shut behind Tyrone.

We're alone, at last.

"So," I say, grinning down at her, unable to conceal my amusement, "still planning on getting that restraining order?"

She sets her jaw, firm and stubborn. "Be pretty hard to get one on my boss."

My smile widens. "Indeed." Without waiting for a

response, I reach down to catch her left wrist, gently disentangling her hands so I can see the left one.

She flinches, and I can tell she wants to pull her hand away, but she's too stubborn for that. I can see it written all over her face, the instant when she decides to just let me do this. That she'll wait. She unclenches her fist, and I gently stretch out her fingers, trying to ignore the flash of memory, back to when these narrow, delicate hands of hers were wrapped around my thick cock.

I pry her left finger up, just an inch, just far enough to spin the ring around and see the diamond. My mother's ring, until my father bought her a newer, bigger, gaudier one. Sometime after I earned my first billion and bailed them both out of debt.

Everyone thinks my family is old money rich. We *used* to be. But through a series of thieving relatives, gambling addictions and even worse alcoholism that my grandparents enjoyed, by the time my parents went on their own spending sprees, there was nothing left for my sister and me. Not even enough to pay for our college educations. So I put myself through school, hell bent on earning enough in whatever career I chose in order to pay for my sister's college next.

I managed that and then some. I even got enough to help my parents out, though they've never thanked me for it.

Their only response has been to pressure me, constantly. Asking about when I'll get engaged, when I'm bringing the lucky lady home, when I'll have a baby to carry on their lineage. *Their* lineage, never mine.

I suppress a smile. My mother would have a heart attack if she knew how this ring got onto this sexy little kitten's finger this weekend.

Then again, my mother would be revived from joy if she

realized that I intend to stick this out. I intend to make this marriage work, if I can. Not for my family, or even to spite them by running off with a girl in Vegas of all places. But because of the way Mara tilts her chin to look at me now, her eyes alight with defiance, even in the face of all the upper hands I have now.

"You're still wearing it," I tell her, softly.

"I couldn't get it off," she replies coolly, gaze narrowed. "Trust me, it doesn't mean anything except that I opted not to find some bolt cutters this morning."

I chuckle, more at the mental image of my mother screaming, watching her ring snapped off by bolt cutters. "Well, it's your ring now," I tell her, not about to explain the complicated history behind it.

Besides, something tells me Mara won't cut it off. Not yet. She's stubborn in the same way that I am. And as much as she hates to admit it, she's realizing now how much we truly have in common.

"So you don't care if I keep this and pawn it?" She arches an eyebrow, considering the diamond anew. "It looks pretty expensive."

"It was," I reply simply. "So does this mean you still want the divorce?"

She snorts, as if I'm joking. When I don't join in, she levels me with another suspicious stare. "Of course. Why wouldn't I?"

"Well." I tilt my head and gesture at the room around us, freshly emptied of employees, but still reeking of power, privilege. And this is the smallest office we have in the building, or any of our buildings. "As you've probably realized by now, I am massively wealthy."

"I don't care about that." She rolls her eyes.

I furrow my brow. "Most people do. Think about it. With

this kind of wealth, you'd never need to work a day in your life."

At that, her hackles rise. She shoves out of her chair, even though standing she still barely comes up to chest height on me. Still, there's something sexy about the way she's trying to take charge, against me of all people. She holds up a finger. "One, I've wanted to work in this industry since childhood, and I have no plans to quit on the first damn day of it. No amount of money would make me just give up on my dreams because they're not *about* money." She pauses to swallow, her jaw still set, her gaze hard on mine. "And two." She lifts a second finger. Now her fingertips tremble, ever so slightly, but just enough to give away the emotion she's trying hard to contain. "I would never take advantage of someone like that. No matter who they were, or how much they irritated me," she adds, probably to disguise the hint of fury sparking in the corners of her eyes.

I take a step closer, unable to tear my gaze from her. I reach up to catch her hand and fold her fingers down, sliding mine between them, until I'm clasping her hand against my chest. She stares at it, then up at me, a crease between her eyebrows that practically begs me to lean in and kiss it until it disappears.

She can't know what she just said. She's proven time and again that she doesn't know a damn thing about me. But still, if she planned to seduce me, to steal more than just my cock—which is definitely already hers, to judge by the near-painful stiffness in my pants—but my heart too... Then she couldn't have come up with a better speech if she tried.

But I'm not ready to broach *that* conversation with her. Not yet.

So I squeeze her hand gently, once more, and release it. "By that logic," I reply, "even if you did get the divorce, we'd

Overnight Wife

still be seeing each other every single day, for hours and hours." I arch an eyebrow. "Since you won't be quitting this job for love or money, and I obviously won't be leaving my own company..."

Her cheeks flush again, and she grimaces like she didn't think about that point.

I shrug one shoulder, playing at being carefree. "So what does the ring really matter then? There's no difference, really, whether you take it off or leave it."

"Why?" she asks, and at first, I don't understand. She shakes her head and tilts her head back, gaze fixed on mine. "Why do you want me to be your wife so badly? You don't know anything about me."

I move in close again, close enough to make her head tilt all the way back in order to keep those soft eyes of hers fixed on my own. I reach up to tuck a single lock of her dark hair behind her ear, my fingers grazing the soft shell of her earlobe just enough to send a shiver down her spine. "I know *some* things about you, Mara," I lean in to whisper, and this time it's not just her spine that shivers, but her whole body.

She leans toward me, her chest grazing mine, just for an instant, but it's enough for me to feel her nipples are rock hard. The way they were our wedding night when she rode me, screaming my name...

God my cock is so fucking hard right now I can barely stand it.

"For example, I cannot stop remembering the look on your face when you come," I murmur, grinning. "Do you know your lips part, and you flush all the way down your chest?" I reach up to brush my fingertip along the underside of her breast, and she gasps, her lips barely inches from mine, and parted now, the same way they do when she comes, yes, just like that. "God, I love watching you come."

Her throat works tightly as she swallows. "I... I never knew I *could* come that hard, until..."

"Until our wedding night?" I lean in. Just another inch and I'll close the gap between us. I can claim that sweet mouth of hers all over again...

"Uh, hello?" A strange woman's voice makes me step back from Mara smoothly. She startles and runs both hands through her hair before reaching down to tug on the hem of her skirt, as if we'd been doing anything. As if that doesn't make it even more obvious what we're trying to hide.

Still, she's adorable in her obviousness. Her whole face is bright red, and she clears her throat hard. "Um, thank you for the... explanation." With that, Mara practically bolts from the room, all while I stand watching her go, torn between amusement and annoyance.

Amusement at Mara. Annoyance at this intrusion.

My cock is still rock fucking hard, but I shift my stance to conceal it better, and take a step until I'm behind the chair Mara was sitting in earlier, helping to conceal my desire and the exact nature of the scene this girl just interrupted.

Then I take in the new girl. I don't recognize her. Blonde hair, done in a tight updo, with a tight pencil skirt and jacket to match. She's cute, albeit not my type. Far too bubbly-looking, like the kind of girl who pays other people to do her hard work, rather than doing it herself.

I prefer women like Mara. Girls who get the job done themselves, who aren't afraid to get their hands dirty.

"Can I help you?" I ask.

She's still flushing too, but her blush isn't nearly as cute as Mara's. It lights up her whole face a bright, unpleasant

Overnight Wife   39

red, and she pats her cheeks a couple times as if she's trying
to calm it down. "Um, sorry, for interrupting." Another
nervous gulp, as if she's thinking again about what she saw.

"Did you need something?" I press, eager to distract her
from the scene she walked in on. My hands grip the chair in
front of me a little tighter.

Her gaze drops to my hands. Specifically my left one,
and I notice her eyes widening with surprise. Now this, I can
tell by her reaction, is a girl who reads tabloids. A girl who
knows how unceremoniously I broke off my previous relationship. Not to mention how recently ago that happened.

She knows I should be single, for all intents and
purposes. And that alone makes me repress another grin. I
do so love knowing more about my own life than the gossip
rags and tabloids do. Staying one step ahead of them, especially when it comes to relationships, is no small feat.

The girl recovers from her shock, somehow. "I'm new
here. Bianca. I missed orientation. I'm sorry, the trains were
running late. It won't happen again, I swear. But they told
me at the front desk that you'd still be in the room and I
should just come in and introduce myself, so I—"

I hold up a hand. I don't like excuses. They bore me. "It's
fine," I tell her. "As long as it doesn't happen again." But I'm
also not without compassion for a new girl on her first day.
"Is there anything else?"

She hesitates. Glances down at my ring, yet again, like
she can't quite help herself. Like she's double checking to
see if she imagined things. "Uh, no, sir, except it's just... I'm
supposed to be one of your assistants, so if there's anything
you need, please let me know and I'm happy to help."

I finger the ring that she won't stop eying. Unlike my
mother's ring, which I gifted to Mara, this one Mara bought
me herself, rather drunkenly, at a pawn shop on the Strip. I

doubt very much that she remembers that point in the night. But she insisted on buying me a ring with her own money, in spite of my protests.

It resulted in the ring I'm wearing, which has already turned my left ring finger an unpleasant shade of green, thanks to the mostly brass core under its cheap gold plating.

I don't care. I don't intend to ever take the damn thing off, no matter if it turns my whole hand green in the end.

I narrow my eyes at Bianca, daring her to comment. But she just forces a bright, bubbly smile and keeps on chattering, about her skills in Excel and how her previous experience as a concierge will help with keeping my schedule in order.

I respond with a bland smile of my own, unable to stop wishing that she was gone, and Mara was back here in this room with me, alone once more.

5

MARA

I can't believe this. This is an actual nightmare. A disaster.

I finally get my dream job. The position I've been working toward my entire life. And I wasn't lying about what I said to John earlier—no amount of money could make me quit this job. But I can't stop running over his words in my head.

You won't be quitting this job for love or money.

Why did he put it that way? The word *love* keeps reverberating through my mind. Chased by his other words. *We'd still be seeing each other every single day, for hours and hours...*

God, I love watching you come.

And the way he backed me up against the wall, his hands drifting over my chest. I could hardly breathe. I knew I should have told him to stop; I should have pushed him away and told him we were ending this marriage, and any potential for a physical relationship between us along with it. But I couldn't do it. I couldn't make my body move, because my damn traitorous body didn't *want* to move.

I wanted his hands all over me.

I wanted him to kiss me until I couldn't think of any reason not to keep kissing him.

I wanted him to pull my skirt up around my waist and fuck me right there in that board room, against the wall of the fancy offices he built from the ground up. I wanted to feel his hands all over my body again, the way they did that night in Vegas, exploring me, touching me, drawing me out until I was putty in his hands, gasping and screaming his name.

I wanted his cock inside me again. And it makes my clit feel heavy with want again now, just to think about it. I'm sure I'm wet, though I'm too nervous to check my panties and make sure.

I suck in a deep breath—then two and three more, trying to steady myself. I'm supposed to be modeling some deer antlers out of clay for the first set project. My direct manager set me up with the kind of workspace I could only dream about in the past, complete with every type of power tool and supply I could possibly dream of, in order to create sets out of my wildest daydreams.

I've got my gloves on, and I'm elbow deep in modeling clay, shaping the antlers, coaxing them out of the mold and into a shape that will be large enough to be seen from the audience, but still a realistic size and complexity for the animal I'm mimicking. But even as I work, I can feel the scrape of this ridiculously huge ring inside the oversized gloves I'm wearing. And all it does is keep dragging my mind away from the task at hand, back in time to the board room where John pinned me against the wall, and where I wish he'd done so much more.

"Help! Somebody!"

I glance up at the sound, startled, and my eyes go wide as they fix on the young man across the room, a guy I

Overnight Wife

vaguely recognize from our new hires meeting, currently pinned on the mold-press machine. It's stamping out patterns for the walls, and his hand is stuck in the brace, the whole contraption currently dragging his fingers, with every deafening stamp, closer to being flattened.

"I can't get loose!" he shouts, and I don't have a second to think.

I drop the antlers—ignoring the crack as the clay, which had already started to harden in some points, breaks apart. Instead, I race across the room and grab the guy's shoulders, yanking him backward hard just before the machine reaches his delicate fingertips.

His hand wrenches free, and he staggers back, until I wrap an arm around his shoulders to catch his full weight. He rebalances after a second, panting, and turns to face me, his whole face bright red. "Thank you," he wheezes, eyes still wide with shock.

"Don't thank me," I tell him, shoving him away none too gently, and reaching past him to snap the emergency release to turn off the machine. It leaves a streak of grease on my gloves, which I wipe against my jeans. "You shouldn't be using that equipment if you don't know the proper safety procedures yet. You could have really hurt yourself."

"I'm sorry." His face, if possible, goes even brighter. "You're right. I just got so eager, and I have one a little bit like this at home, so I figured I could guess... But the trapping mechanism is different, and—" He stops himself. "Doesn't matter. Thanks. I won't try that again."

I roll my eyes. "Let me show you how it really works," I say, pulling off my gloves one at a time. I'm about to demonstrate the proper usage of the machine when the doors to the workroom slide open, and a blonde girl around my age steps inside. There's something familiar about her. It takes me a second to place her as the girl who walked in on me and John earlier, and my whole face flares bright red, though I suck in a deep breath in order to try and conceal it.

As for her, she doesn't seem to have noticed anything. If she recognizes me, at least she's too professional to let it show right now, something for which I'm deeply grateful. "Did I hear someone shouting help?" she asks.

I point my thumb at the guy, who ducks his head and introduces himself as Daniel. "I was using the machine wrong. She was just about to show me the proper way."

"Mara," I add, sticking my hand out to shake first Daniel's and then this new girl's hand.

"Bianca," she answers. "Do you need any help?" Her eyes skitter around the room and then land on the disaster that used to be my carefully sculpted antlers. It's half a pile of unfinished mushy clay and half a pile of shattered antler ends that will be melted down and remolded after I'm finished helping Daniel. "Maybe I could clean up a bit."

"That'd be great, thanks," I tell her. She sets off to clean up my area while I instruct Daniel on the proper usage of this tool. To his credit, after that initial mishap at least, he seems to be paying very close attention to every single thing I say. He even takes out a notepad to jot down some of the more important steps. By the time I finish explaining it to him, I'm at the very least not worried that he's going to accidentally take his fingers off.

It's still to be determined whether he can work the thing well enough to get some decent designs out of it, especially the kind of delicately shaped ones we'll need for this particular set, which is half a hunting lodge (hence my antler designs) and half an outdoor scene, which will need not only trees and branches and a forest, but also stars and the moon overhead. It'll be a tricky set to pull off without

Overnight Wife

crossing over into cheesy territory. The last thing we want is to look like some high schooler's play with second-rate set designs. I'm pretty sure none of us would last more than a couple weeks on the job if we turned out something like that—no matter how much of an in we might have with the boss.

The thought of that makes my stomach flip again, and I can't help but steal another glance over at Bianca, who's moved on to tidying the rest of the room after she finished sweeping up my antler mess. *Does she know what she saw? Did she figure out it was me?*

As if my situation couldn't get any more awkward or embarrassing.

Bianca catches me staring at her and smiles, heading over to my side like I summoned her. Maybe I did. I'm still not really sure how this whole setup works. I know I'm supposed to have a couple of assistants on my team reporting to my same manager, to help out with tasks I set them. But I'm not sure if Bianca is one of them, or if she's just so eager to prove herself on day one that she doesn't care who's giving her jobs as long as she can complete them.

"What should I do next? Anything more you need?" she asks, and I bite the inside of my lip, considering.

"Not sure. Er... do you have the time to help? I don't want to keep you, if you have other duties..."

She shrugs and spreads her hands wide with a *what can you do* sort of laugh. "I'm not sure yet. Mr. Walloway is supposed to be giving me an assignment, but he told me he wouldn't have anything put together until tomorrow, so he just said to help out for now..."

The sound of John's last name makes my heart skitter in my chest all over again. *How could I be this stupid?* I'd googled John Walloway a thousand times before now, obviously. But

I only ever read his work profiles, interviews about how he started this company and why. Those interviews, in magazines like the *New Yorker* and *Economist* almost never included photos—or if they did, they were moody Steve Jobs-esque photos in profile, where you could hardly make out John's face, let alone any identifying features. It never even occurred to me to google pictures of the guy himself. Why would I? I figured he'd be some higher up I'd see but never actually speak to around the office.

Someone I'd eventually want to get to know, to have know *me*, but not... *Not in the way you did, you idiot.* My inner critic hasn't stopped lambasting me all day. Of all the guys I could choose for a random Vegas hook up—let alone *marriage*....

But I force those thoughts from my head, hoping that Bianca won't read too much into the extremely pregnant pause hovering in the air between us now. "Hmm, well, I don't have too many more jobs around here, unless you want to help me melt down that clay and start reshaping a new set of antler designs—"

"Sure!" Bianca perks up right away, which makes my eyebrows rise.

"You really don't have to."

"Don't be silly." She elbows me. "I'd love to help. Sounds more fun than all the desk work I'll be doing soon anyway, right?" Her smile is so open and earnest, I can't bring myself to question it.

So together we cross over to the ovens and set about putting together some new clay molds that I can shape into the huge antler sets we'll need. As we work, we chat about our backgrounds and how we got started at Pitfire. Unlike me, Bianca comes from a marketing background, so she's not interested in the actual set design part of what we're

Overnight Wife   47

doing here. But she talks a lot about how much she admires "Mr. Walloway"'s business strategies, and how she really wanted the assistant job so she could learn from him about getting ahead at work.

"If there's anyone who can teach a girl how to rise up through the world with the cards stacked against us ladies, it's him, right?"

I stifle a smirk. "Why, because he had so many cards stacked against him?" I roll my eyes. "Isn't his whole family wealthy?"

"You didn't read the profile they did of him in *Vogue*?" Bianca's gaze sharpens, then widens in disbelief when I shake my head. "Well, his family lost all their money when he was young. He's the one who pulled them all out of borderline poverty—paid for his younger sister to go to college and bailed out his parents from huge debt, too."

My eyebrows go up. I can't help but feel a tiny pang in my chest, a shift, as I realign my opinions of the man I mistakenly married, just a little. *Maybe he's not entirely the rich cocky businessman he seems.* Okay, no, he's *definitely* still cocky. But maybe there's more to him than just that.

Maybe you haven't given him a real chance.

But even that thought is insane. How can I give a guy I accidentally eloped with a chance at marriage, when I barely know him? Much less when he's my boss, and as he himself pointed out, we're going to have to work in close proximity for... well, hopefully for a very long time, if my career plans pan out.

"You really don't know much about him?" Bianca's brow furrows, and I shake my head with a shrug.

"What can I say? We don't talk much." I pull off my gloves absently, about to go and wash my hands at the sink, having finished sculpting one half of the antlers we'll need,

48   PENNY WYLDER

and figuring now will be as good a time as any to call a
lunch break for the shop.

But Bianca stops me with a single question. "How long
have you been married?"

My heart jump starts in my chest. My veins turn to ice.
How does she know? I think, my pulse racing, afraid she'll use
this against me, or spread rumors around the water cooler...

But then I notice her gaze fixed down, on the ring I'd
forgotten was still attached like a limpet to my left ring
finger, and my muscles relax. *Oh.* All she saw was the ring.
She doesn't know about me and John.

Well, unless she saw more this morning than she's been
letting on. Still, I clear my throat, and force the easiest smile
possible onto my face. "Oh, uh..." I can't tell the truth. It's
too humiliating. And it's the last thing I want all my new
coworkers to think about me: that I married John for his
money, or that John only hired me because I'm his latest
fling, his new Vegas wife. "Not too long. It's pretty new. Keep
forgetting this is here," I add, laughing, a little bit edgily,
though at least Bianca doesn't seem to notice.

"That's great." She smiles and sighs a little wistfully. "I
want to marry young, too. I just think there's no point in
waiting until you're all old and gray, right? Might as well
have kids early, so you can have more fun with them when
they're grown up with you."

My stomach flips. I never thought about that. I never
gave much thought to kids, period. I mean, I think I want
them eventually. But it always seemed like such a far-off
possibility, something to worry about years and years down
the line.

Not something I might have to consider now. Much less
after one drunken night of blowing off steam in Sin City.

I force myself to smile. "Yeah, I guess so. I hadn't really

Overnight Wife   49

thought about kids yet, but... good point." Bianca grins back
at me, and I nod toward the clock. "Lunch?" I ask, mostly to
change the subject. To my relief, she nods, and she and
Daniel file out, leaving me to unpack the lunch I brought
with me from home.

I eat in silence and get back to work quickly. Thanks to
all the stopping and starting, I'm much farther behind than
I hoped I'd be by the end of the day. I'm still sculpting when
Daniel clocks out and Bianca waves goodbye, off to go get
some actual office assignments from John himself.

I'm still sculpting when in a far end of the shop,
someone flicks off the light.

"Still here," I call, and footsteps approach, the light
flicking back on. I don't turn around or look up from my
project—I'm at a particularly delicate part of the procedure,
trying to attach one set of antlers to the base of another. I
hold my breath, leaning in, just about to make the
connection...

"You're behind."

My stomach plummets. Luckily, I catch my hands before
they shake too much, and I'm able to finish pressing the two
halves together, the seriously heavy-duty glue I used making
them stick. I grip them while the glue finishes processing,
and glance over my shoulder toward John, who's standing at
my back, arms folded, a cocksure grin on his face that both
annoys me and sends a bolt of desire straight to my core.

Fuck. I still want him.

But that's to be expected. It doesn't change anything.

It doesn't mean I can have him.

"I had to save someone's hands earlier," I respond curtly,
refocusing on my work.

He chuckles.

"Not a joke," I add. "You really should have more strict

safety guidelines introduced before you let people start running around playing with these machines."

"I had you here," he replies, coming over to lean against my table, in my line of sight this time. "Seems like you had it all under control, from what Bianca tells me."

I shoot him a narrowed glare. "Did you send your secretary to spy on me?"

"Hardly." He chuckles. "She seems to have wanted to do that all on her own. I wonder why. It's almost as if she seems jealous of you about something..."

I roll my eyes with a grimace. "You wish."

"I don't have to." His hand drops over mine, his fingertips finding the ring and toying with it easily. He's barely touching me, his palm only skimming the back of my hand, yet already it feels like my whole body is on fire, leaning into that touch, yearning for more, more, *more.*

I suck in a breath, which catches at the back of my throat, both of our gazes fixed on my finger. On the ring, and everything it represents. All the insane, stupid, wild choices we made.

I take another breath, not sure what I'm about to ask— whether I want to ask him to step back and give me more room... Or come closer and wipe away the space between our bodies entirely. Already, my helpful imagination is providing visions of him sweeping a hand across my desk to clear it before he bends me over, his hands running up my sides, down to my hips, gripping me hard, his lips searing across mine again...

Before I can say anything, though, before I can give in and suggest such a terrible idea, he steps back from me on his own, a smirk on his face. And what he says next, I couldn't have predicted.

"Do you need some help?"

Overnight Wife 51

It takes me a second to understand what he means. To see the way he nods toward the almost-finished antlers on the desk.

When he does, my eyebrows lift even higher. "You know how?"

He laughs at that, long and low. "I realize I'm a CEO now, but I didn't start out that way," he points out. "I had to learn this business working at other companies, before I started Pitfire." He turns away from me, but only to cross to where I've been keeping the unformed clay. He scoops out a healthy handful, then strides back to the table and pulls up a stool beside me, starting to work the clay between his palms. "I did a lot of prop-making in my early days. I used to love it, actually."

I watch him knead, distracted by the steady, sure motions of his hands. Watching his hands clench and release, and those long, strong fingers of his dig into the clay, it's impossible not to think about how his hands felt when they were all over *me* instead.

Goddamn it. I'm getting wet just sitting next to him— close enough to smell that musky cologne of his, dark and heady—and watching his hands work. I am so fucking screwed, if I think I'm going to be able to work here every day and never give in to him…

I drive the thoughts from my mind with effort. *One day at a time.* I'm pretty sure that's what they tell people about how to get over addictions, but it feels fitting in this situation too, worryingly.

Then John catches me watching, and I tear my eyes away, my cheeks burning. "Did you always want to work in this industry?" I ask, just for something, anything to say. To guide our conversation to work topics and my mind away from sexier thoughts.

He doesn't. He just smiles, a sly little half-grin that tells me he knows exactly what I'm thinking, damn him. "It's always been my passion. For a while, though, I was looking into other career paths. Not usually a lot of money in this one, not unless you're incredible at it."

"Lucky you turned out to be," I reply with a smirk.

"Luck had nothing to do with it," he answers, his dark eyes glittering in the overhead light. I'm reminded all over again how much he and I have in common when it comes to our work ethics.

After that, we work in silence for a stretch. I finish the rest of the antler set I'm working on, and John starts the final one. Eventually, I pitch in to join him on his, and while we work, we talk a little about our families. He talks about his sister mostly—she went to college for architecture, and she just started working at some fancy firm in Paris. I talk about my mom being proud of me for what I'm doing now. I purposefully don't mention Dad, afraid of what talking about him will do to me, but John catches the absence, and asks.

"Your father isn't proud?"

My throat tightens around a sudden lump, but I force my way through it. After all, it's been two years. I need to get used to this eventually, don't I? "He probably would be, if he knew. He, uh... he died, a couple years back." The lump sits there, stubborn, preventing me from saying anything else.

John reaches over to catch my hand, squeezing gently, just enough pressure to let me know he's here. "I'm so sorry."

I clear my throat, hard. Then again. "I was closer to him than Mom. More of a daddy's girl, you know." I glance around the shop, inadvertently looking toward the machinery Daniel almost injured himself on earlier. "Dad's

Overnight Wife

the one who taught me how to use most of the stuff in this room, actually. We used to build things together in the garage downstairs. Well, he was always building useful stuff, repairing cars... I was just making useless crap. Decorations and toy swords and stuff."

John laughs at the mental image. "He sounds great."

"He was."

Another silence passes, this one more companionable than our last, filled with less tension. It's the first time I've talked to anyone, including Lea, about my father without immediately bursting into tears. Something about chatting with John is just easy, even when it comes to subjects like this.

Something tells me Dad would have liked him, if they'd ever gotten a chance to meet.

I drive that thought from my mind, my eyes jumping guiltily to the ring I'm wearing. Dad would've *killed* me if he'd ever found out *how* John and I met, actually. Scratch that. He'd probably just kill John and bury the body somewhere far away, then tell me I was grounded until my mid-thirties.

The thought brings a smile to my face.

John catches it, and smiles back, and there's something way too familiar about this scene. Almost like we've been here before, done this before. "Hungry?" John asks.

I blink, confused by the question. But my stomach growls in response, actually audible in the dead quiet studio, which makes us both laugh. "I guess that answers that," I say.

"Come on." John pats the finishing touches onto his own set of antlers and then offers me a hand up from the table. "Let's go grab a bite to eat."

My eyes dart toward the clock on the far wall. "I don't

54   PENNY WYLDER

know. It's so late..." *Already almost 10pm. When did that happen?* Last I'd checked the clock was two hours ago. But time flew while John and I were talking, I guess.

"Exactly." John extends an elbow, ever the gentleman. "You need food, and I need to make sure you get home safe. Perfect solution." I hesitate, but he must sense that I'm close to caving in, because he flashes me a wink. "I won't take no for an answer."

With a sigh that turns into a groan, I reach out and hook my arm through his. "Now who's the stubborn one?" I grumble. But still, I trail him out into the parking lot, unable to resist.

6

MARA

"Wow." I was expecting an expensive car, but not... *this*. "Is this a Veneno?" I ask as John hits the switch to open the passenger side door of his Lamborghini. "I thought these were limited edition." I run a hand along the edge of the car, unable to resist, before I climb inside. "Aren't there only like... ten of these in the world?"

The interior is almost as breathtaking as the exterior.

"Nine, actually." He grins as he taps a button to seal us both into the car. It looks like he's starting up a spaceship, and I lean over eagerly to watch him do it. His smile widens when he catches me watching. "You know a lot about cars?"

"A little more than average, I'd say." I run my hands across the dash, eyeing the controls. "You ever let anybody else drive this?"

He laughs softly. "I'd probably have to let my wife, wouldn't I?"

My breath hitches, not just at the promise, but also at the reminder. I lean back with effort and put on my seat belt, trying not to let my hands tremble, or thoughts of what we're doing here, of who we are to each other, invade my mind. "Y'know, it might be worth this whole mess, actually," I respond, surprising both myself and him into laughter.

But then his gaze turns sly as he flashes me a long, considering look. "I'm sure I can think of a few other ways to make this all worth it," he points out.

Before I can respond to that, he pulls out onto the highway and really lets the car do its thing. For a moment, my breath is caught in my throat, and I lean forward, eager to experience this. I've never been in a car like this. We weave between the usual LA snarl of traffic effortlessly. I swear, the cars we pass stop or slow to let us ahead, staring while we pass.

Well, except for the couple of BMWs who cut us off. But that's BMW drivers for you.

By the time we're slowing down on a side street, we're both grinning, breathless. I expect John to take me to some hole-in-the-wall, the kind of place that will be open this late, not to mention open to us rolling up in our paint-and-clay-covered work clothes. It's not exactly a work environment where you can pop out to a nice restaurant after a day of work.

But instead, John pulls up to one of the most expensive restaurants in town—one I recognize from magazine articles like "Where LA's A-Listers Eat." Lea's always interested in magazines like that, and I usually make fun of her because when would girls like us *ever* get the chance to eat at places like *that*?

And yet here I am.

"We can't go here," I protest as we pull to a stop and John hits the button to open our doors. It feels like climbing out of a spaceship. So I stay seated and glare at him instead.

"Why, because we don't have a reservation?" He chuckles. "Relax. They know me." He climbs out of the car and

Overnight Wife

circles around to my side, but it only makes me more determined not to step out and embarrass myself.

I cross my arms over my chest to hide the paint stains up both of my arms. "We're not dressed for this," I hiss. "Look at me!"

"I am." He leans on the side of the car and grins down at me, his eyes taking me in slowly, an inch at a time like I'm a meal he's savoring. "And you look absolutely flawless to me. I don't see the problem."

My face flushes with heat. But I shake my head, refusing to be swayed by his flattery. "You might find paint splatter cute, but I promise you, most people at a restaurant like this won't."

"I don't care about what most think." He reaches in to take my hand, forcibly prying my arms apart, before he tugs on them, lifting me from the car.

Reluctantly, I climb out of it next to him and shoot him another glare, an angrier one this time. I hope. But if I'm expecting that to deter him, I am sadly mistaken.

In fact, the next thing I know, he's scooped me up into his arms.

I gasp and push at his chest. "What are you doing?"

He just squeezes me tighter against him, and I can't deny, the feeling of his strong, muscular arms wrapped around me, cradling me against his hard chest, is reassuring. "It might not count as a threshold, but I'm pretty sure it's tradition to carry your wife into the first place you're going to share a meal together, isn't it?"

I groan and roll my eyes, not that it does any good in terms of deterring him. I catch the sound of a chuckle, and spot the valet over John's shoulder, having already accepted the keys from John, watching this whole spectacle with amusement.

In fact, quite a lot of people are watching, now that I'm looking.

John just tightens his hold on me and starts toward the stairs. "Your choice," he says. "What do you think will be more embarrassing, walking in on your own two feet, covered in paint, or being carried in?" He is getting way too much enjoyment out of this.

"Both," I grumble. "Both are embarrassing." Behind us, a handful of other people on dates, all dressed to the nines, stare and point. Somewhere, a camera flashes. Great. Someone's probably recognized John Walloway. "And everyone's staring at us," I hiss.

"Good," he replies, not at all what I expect. But he sets me down, at least, at the top of the staircase, before we reach the actual hostess stand. Not that it makes any difference at this point. Half the restaurant saw us through the broad windows that look out over the street. "I want people to see us together," he murmurs, leaning in closer, so his chin is tucked against my temple, his breath caressing my skin. "I want them to know you're mine."

My belly flutters at those words, my skin prickling with electricity all over again, the same way it did when he was holding me against his warm, strong chest. His hand traces down my arm until his fingers thread through mine, and I can't help it, I squeeze his hand in response, remembering just how good this man is with his hands. All the sounds and screams he coaxed out of me, before...

My cheeks flush with heat, but luckily, we've reached the hostess stand now, and there's no time to indulge the embarrassment.

John asks for a table, and the hostess doesn't even ask about a reservation. She just flashes him a smile, the kind that tells me she knows exactly who he is. People have

Overnight Wife

different smiles they use on rich, wealthy people. "Your usual table, Mr. Walloway?" the hostess asks.

"I've told you, you can call me John," he says amiably, though he tugs me forward, and we trail after her through the restaurant.

"So you have, Mr. Walloway," she responds, and it catches me off guard enough to make me chuckle. The hostess glances my way, something new in her expression now—curiosity.

I realize, too late, what all this means. John taking me to a place where he's a regular, where people will see us, and know him.

I want them to know you're mine.

He's trying to make this marriage a public thing. With this huge ring on my finger, people won't fail to start whispering about my appearance here with him.

It should irritate me. Piss me off, even. But there's something hot about it. About how eager he is to claim me, and how he doesn't seem to care about the consequences.

We're barely seated before another server appears, and the bartender quickly behind him, dropping a pair of cocktails we didn't order on our table.

"A new drink I'm testing," the bartender explains, his eyes on John. "I'd like your opinion on it."

"Of course." John smiles, and the words are barely out of his mouth before an appetizer appears next.

"Compliments of the chef," the waiter explains, before he vanishes.

We lean back in our seats, and I watch the waitstaff continue to fuss over him, my amusement growing with every passing moment. Finally, when the attention settles down, and we're alone at our table with a heap of food and drinks we never ordered, I raise my glass. "Do you like this, then?" I ask.

"The food? You'll love it," he says. "It's sublime."

"Being treated like a king," I correct, with a nod toward his plate, already heaped with the first course—the chef's selection based on John's tastes and preferences. Which, of course, they already know.

There's a long pause, during which I flash a glance at him, wondering if I've struck a nerve.

But far from looking annoyed, John only seems pensive. Then he chuckles under his breath. "You know, I'm so used to being treated like this, I forget..."

I arch an eyebrow. "What, you think everybody gets this kind of treatment wherever they go?"

He shakes his head. "I just forget it's not common, that's all."

"Believe me, I have *never* had anyone fuss over me this much," I respond with a laugh.

But that makes his face shift into a more serious expression. "Well then, I'll have to change that, won't I?" he says softly. At the same time, his hand slides over to me, concealed beneath the long tablecloth. His palm comes to rest over my knee, squeezing gently, just hard enough to send a spark through my veins.

It's enough to make me jump, that sudden contact, the unexpected touch. When I do, I'm still holding my cocktail in hand, the one I've yet to take a sip of, so it's filled nearly to the brim. It splashes out across the tablecloth and my lap, making me gasp.

But John just grins, unrepentant, as I pat myself dry. "Yes. We're definitely going to need to get you accustomed to being spoiled."

My cheeks flush with heat again, and I manage to flash

Overnight Wife   61

him a glare. "If it winds up with me spilling half my drinks in my lap, then I'd rather not, thanks," I reply.

He only laughs and lifts his own glass in a toast.

When I do manage to actually try a sip of the cocktail rather than throwing it across myself, it's delicious. Light and fruity, with just a hint of alcohol... That's the kind of thing that could prove dangerous. Not like those shots we were doing in Vegas where you feel every burning sip of the booze. No. This is a sleeper drink, the kind where you don't even notice you're drinking it until suddenly you're drunk.

I set it aside, resolved not to drink too much around John. Not again. God knows what would happen this time. We'd probably wind up buying a house, or with me getting pregnant.

My cheeks flush bright red at the thought. *Why am I thinking about babies all of a sudden?* I have got to stop this. I must be ovulating or something.

Still, the thought leads to thinking about how that baby would get made, which leads to yet more flashbacks to the last time he and I were completely naked together, in the most expensive hotel room I've ever seen, but far too focused on each other to even notice our surroundings...

I clear my throat, mostly to get those memories out of my head. When I glance up, I find John watching me closely.

"Why were you in Vegas last weekend?" he asks, and I swear it's like this man can read my mind sometimes. I wonder if he learned how to do that in business school or if my face is too easy to read.

Or maybe he just gets me, adds a voice in my head. The way nobody else I've ever met has seemed to...

"Oh, I..." I shrug one shoulder. "It was on a dare. Lea wanted me to let loose, have some fun for once."

He chuckles. "Ah, so I'll have to thank her the next time I see her." He flashes me his own left hand, and my eyes widen. Somehow, in all the time that's passed since that weekend, I hadn't really noticed *his* ring. But there it is, a band of gold with... is that a layer of green beneath?

I frown. There's something familiar about that... Something that brings back a flash of fuzzy memory from the weekend, something I'd all but forgotten. A pawn shop, dingy lighting, but we were too drunkenly happy to care, laughing it all off. And... "Wait, did I give that to you?" I ask.

"Give is a rather nice word." He laughs. "Don't you remember how hard you struggled to force it onto my finger?"

I grimace. That doesn't sound familiar, yet it sounds sadly believable, given the state I was in. "Sorry. Clearly I couldn't afford actual gold." I hold out a hand and he lets me take his hand, tracing my fingers over the metal. I glance up at him, my cheeks bright red again, for reasons I can't quite put a name to now. "You don't have to wear it, you know," I say.

"I know," he replies, those dark eyes fixed on mine, inscrutable, impossible to tear my gaze away from. "But I want to," he says, so simply that it feels like a bolt to my chest, a spark of sheer desire that ignites me.

He wants to. This wealthy as hell billionaire businessman, who could have anyone and anything in the world he wanted, wants to wear the shitty, green ring that I bought him in a pawn shop.

"Where did you get this one?" I ask, with a smile, fingering the ring on my own hand next. "The same shop, or did we do a pawn shop hop all down the strip searching?"

Something flashes across his face. Hesitation? But it's

Overnight Wife 63

gone the moment I glimpse it. "That was my mother's ring," he says, and whatever answer I expected, it isn't that.

My stomach does a strange little flip of desire, and my thighs tighten, as I consider the ring in a whole new light. "But..."

He shakes his head. "She gave it to me years ago. Family heirloom. I usually carry it with me as a sort of good luck token, but after we met, well... it seemed like the right moment to part with it."

My throat works tightly when I swallow. "How does your mother feel about it?" I ask, not sure whether I want to know the answer just yet. *Did he tell her about us?* "About you giving this to someone you barely know, I mean."

"I didn't tell her yet," he answers, simply as that, his gaze still fixed on mine.

It's the *yet* that catches me. "Why not?"

"I want you to meet her."

I snort. He just stares at me, and I realize he wasn't kidding. "*Meet* her? What, like this is an actual..." I shake my head. "We barely know each other, John. And now, you're my boss, it's not proper, there's—"

"We were married before you started working for me." He waves a hand, as if that wave can make all the worries fade away. "And I don't give a damn about propriety. I know what I want. Do you?"

"I..." I clamp my mouth shut. *No. I have no idea.* That's what I want to say, but I stop myself.

It doesn't seem to matter. He can read it all over my face, just like he can read everything. All my moods, as easily as if I were a neon sign. His expression shifts, hurt flashing across his face briefly, and it settles in my gut like a stone.

I hurt him. Why does it feel so terrible? Why do I wish I

could just reach across the table between us and wipe the frown off his face?

But I can't. Because I don't know what I want yet. An annulment or... No. That's the only choice. The only option. The only sane thing I *can* want is an annulment, just like we said from the start.

Luckily, I'm temporarily saved from replying as the waiter stops by our table with another course, followed quickly by the bartender asking our opinion on the new cocktails. It temporarily saves me from having to think about that brief flash of hurt on John's face. From wondering why, deep down, a little part of me is starting to question... *What if we* didn't *fix this?*

But that's crazy talk. Isn't it?

7

JOHN

I wait until our audience clears out again before I reach back beneath the table to cup Mara's knee again. She feels so soft beneath my touch, even through the fabric of her jeans—such a contrast to her hands, which, like mine, are rough with callouses. I love those contrasts in her. Smooth and hard, soft and stubborn. She's like no one I've ever met, except for maybe myself.

She'll see that soon. She'll realize this is meant to be.

I just have to make her see it.

Even now, as I caress her leg, my fingers slowly inching upward, she doesn't pull away from me like she would have before. She goes still, and lets me touch her, hand wandering higher, higher.

"I don't want to hide this, Mara," I say softly, and she leans toward me, her body responding even when her mind tries to refuse.

"Hide what?" she murmurs, her gaze distracted, her eyes half focused on the table, her mind surely stuck underneath it, where my fingers have reached almost the top of her inner thigh, the fabric warm from her skin, searing hot against my palm. I dig my fingers in a little harder, make her lips part in an almost gasp, before I let my fingertips rest along the crease of her jeans, ever so lightly.

She shifts in her seat, pushing a little toward my hand, even as she tries to hold herself back.

"I want the world to know you're my wife," I say, and at that moment, I give her what she wants. I press down harder, my fingertips rubbing against the denim, sending friction straight to her clit.

She gasps, and clutches at the edge of the tablecloth, pulling it over her lap even further, as if that will make it less obvious what's happening here.

It makes me grin. She can be so naïve at times. So worldly at others. Full of contradictions, my wife.

"Why?" she breathes, her voice coming quick and low. "Why would you want that?" Her gaze finds mine, her eyes wide and blue and filled with questions. Questions, and something else. A searing heat that I recognize from our wedding night together.

She wants me, just as badly as I want her.

Which is going to make this all the more fun. I smile. "Because I'm selfish," I tell her. "When I decide I want something, I can't bear the thought of losing it. And when it comes to *you*, well..." I shift my fingers against her, three of them now, rubbing her through the fabric of her pants. "I don't want anyone even *thinking* they can take you from me. You're mine, Mara."

She arches up in her seat, pushing against me in spite of herself, her breath coming faster, her face and her chest both flushed that lovely shade of crimson I so enjoy drawing out of her. "But... Aren't you worried it will be... embarrassing? If we... if it... if the marriage fails..." Her breath starts to stutter as I continue to stroke her, slow and steady, never

Overnight Wife   67

enough to take her all the way to orgasm. Just enough to edge her closer and closer to the peak.

"It won't fail," I reply simply. "You're my wife. Now. Forever. That's how marriage works, isn't it?"

"But this... but we..." She can't muster up the argument. Not with how dizzy she is from what I'm doing to her under this table right now.

What I don't expect, however, is for her to turn the tables on me. The next thing I know, her palm is flat against my lap, her fingers tracing the hard, thick bulge against the seam of my jeans, where I'm already hard just from thinking about her, sitting across from her, watching her lick a drop of her cocktail from her upper lip.

Everything about this woman drives me wild, in the best possible way. And I don't want it to stop.

I don't want any of this to stop.

So as her fingers inch around me, stroking me hesitantly at first, then more firmly, I stretch out my free hand to flag the waitstaff casually.

I pay, even as I reach over to catch the back of Mara's chair and slide her close to me. "I can't wait any longer," I whisper against her neck, my lips finding her skin, tasting her, touching her. I trail my tongue up along the crease of her neck, up to her ear, which makes her whole body shiver deliciously against mine. "I need to have you again, wife."

Another shiver, this time elicited by that one word alone. It thrills me, how much power I have over her, just from that simple term. It makes me want to get her out of here, into my car, somewhere where I can call her that again and again until she's screaming "husband" in return.

The very thought makes my grin turn wolfish.

I sign the bill in a heartbeat, and in the next, I pull us both up out of our seats. I scoop her into my arms once more, against her protests and groans about embarrassment. But this time, I need to carry her in order to hide the raging hard-on she's given me, so she can hardly complain. I tell her so and enjoy the new flush on her cheeks as she bows her head against my chest, giving up, at least for the moment.

It lasts until we're outside. Only then do I let her down onto her own two feet, but only long enough so that I can pin her against the wall of the restaurant, and do what I've been hungry to do ever since I saw her this morning—ever since we were torn apart by that intrusion at work.

I kiss her, hard and deep, my tongue slipping between her lips, my hands circling her waist. She arches up against me, with a soft little sigh of relief that makes me growl in response, because *fuck,* I want her. I want to claim every inch of this gorgeous, sexy, hard as nails woman.

I push her against the wall, and she raises one leg, just far enough that I grab under her thigh and yank her against me. My cock is so hard I'm sure she can feel it, even through the thick fabric of both my jeans and her own. My mouth leaves hers to trail down her neck, kissing and sucking and nipping at her skin, savoring the taste of her, salty and sweet all at once, with a hint of something light and floral, not quite perfume. Maybe the scent of her shampoo? Whatever it is, I love it. I can't get enough.

I drink her in, tracing my hands down her sides, over the smooth planes of her curves. She shivers under my hands, and I grin down at her.

"See? It's not so bad going public, is it?"

Her breath hitches then, and she glances to one side, only just now noticing what I knew all along. We've got an audience. Several other diners from the restaurant, and a handful more who hadn't entered yet, all staring open-

Overnight Wife   69

mouthed. The stares only grow more pronounced when the valet responds and tosses me back the keys. I flash Mara a jaunty wink and head toward the car, leaving her to rearrange her shirt, which had ridden up far enough in all the fuss to show a thin line of her pale stomach.

When she manages, she jogs after me, still glaring as she climbs into the passenger seat beside mine. "You did that on purpose," she mutters.

"I told you, I won't hide you, or this marriage."

"But *why*?"

I reach across to trace her knee again, and she shivers, even despite all her protesting. "Why do you keep fighting this, I think is the more interesting question, Mara."

"I never thought about having a husband," she replies. "I want a career, not... not marriage."

"Why not have both?" I arch one eyebrow. "I fully intend to."

Her breath catches again, but when I steal a glance at her, just as I start up the car and pull away from the curb, it doesn't seem to be because she's resisting. She honestly looks like she hadn't considered the possibility.

"I... don't know. It's always been an either-or proposition," she says. "Either a husband and family or a career. I want the career."

"Don't limit yourself like that." I shrug. And the look on her face tells me she's never considered that point of view, either.

I don't drive us far. One exit away, and then I'm swinging off the highway already, aimed toward the nearest dark alley.

"Where are we going?" she asks, her hands still tracing my forearm absently, as if she wants to pull me toward her, make me start touching her again, but she doesn't quite have the guts to go for what she wants yet.

I flash her another grin, sly this time. "I can't wait," I say. I put the car into park at the mouth of the first dark, empty alleyway I can find, and grab both her hips, drawing her toward me. "I need you. Now."

She hesitates, but only long enough to undo her seatbelt. And then she's swinging her free leg across mine, straddling my lap, and I reach up to cup her face between my palms and pull her down into another hard kiss. While she's distracted, I reach down to undo the clasp on her jeans and push them down past her ass.

She gasps, glancing out and around the car, worried someone will see us. But I just chuckle and hit a button on the dash, making the windows instantly darken around us.

"Relax," I tell her, eyes alight with amusement. "I don't plan on sharing *every* aspect of our marriage with the world."

She arches an eyebrow, amused. "Just the part where you touch me under the table in the nicest restaurant in the city?"

I scoff. "That hardly counted. I wasn't about to make you come right there."

"How do you know?" She tilts her head, frowning.

My smile widens. "Because, my darling, you not only have an incredibly sensitive, tight pussy." I emphasize this by sliding one palm under her panties and cupping her bare, clean-shaven mound. "But you are so very easy to read, too." I stroke her with my thumb, in slow circles, just above her clit, which I can already tell is aroused as hell thanks to my touching her earlier in the restaurant. "I know exactly how to get every response I want out of your body, if you let me," I tell her.

Overnight Wife   71

At that, she arches into my palm, her hips twisting as she grinds against me, her breath coming shorter, faster.

I smile and slide my hand back out, making her twist to a halt, her lips still parted with frustration. Her throat works around a hard swallow, as she clearly bites back her instinctive response, to ask me to keep going.

Then she surprises me. She reaches down between us to cup the hard bulge in my jeans, her fingers digging into the seams a little, pressing around me. She shifts her palm back and forth, and I grit my teeth to stop a low, guttural sound from escaping.

The feel of her small hands on my cock only makes me harder. It makes me want to torment her more.

"Eager, are you, my darling?" I arch an eyebrow, and she pauses, her eyes narrowing.

"You're the one who teased me throughout dinner."

"Teased you?" I chuckle, completely unrepentant, and reach up to take her waist. In one swift move, I spin her around, leaning my seat back at the same time, so she's pinned underneath me on the driver's seat. "That was nothing." I lean in to kiss my way down the side of her neck. When I reach the hem of her shirt, I slide one hand up underneath it, my fingertips tracing the warm plane of her stomach, up over her curves until they reach the underside of her breasts. Her bra is tight, but I trace around the back of it, my hands following the smooth, silky feeling fabric until I find the clasp.

"I know you know how to beg, my lovely wife." I grin down at her. "I intend to hear you do it again."

She breathes in sharply as I undo her bra clasp, tugging it off from beneath her shirt. Then, gently, I push her shirt up and out of the way, before my mouth continues its attack.

I trail my tongue down the center of her chest first,

following the trail between her breasts, tasting her salty, sweet flavor. At the same time, I cup both her breasts in my hot palms, kneading them gently, her nipples beginning to harden against the flat of my palm.

When she starts to breathe a little faster, I run my thumbs across them, pressing down just hard enough to make the hard little nubs swell beneath the pads of my thumbs. I tilt my face to one side and gently nip at the soft, sensitive skin below her nipples.

She gasps, then sinks into a moan as I suck at the spot now, my lips soothing the bite before I nip her again, a little closer to the nipple.

Both her nipples are rock hard by the time I suck one into my mouth, my tongue toying with her sensitive bud, rolling back and forth across her until her back arches up off the seat.

At the same time, my hands slide down her waist, over the incline of her hips, my fingers digging in just enough to make her twist closer to me, pressing in, eager for the touch. My fingertips reach the hem of her jeans, and I slip beneath them again, toying with the edge of her panties as I shift my mouth to her other breast, licking and sucking until she's moaning, her breath harder, faster.

I tilt my head back and grin up at her. "Tell me you want your husband to fuck you," I say.

Her throat works hard with a tight gulp. "I... that's not... fair," she manages, her eyes darkening.

I tilt my head with a smirk and shrug one shoulder. "Your call. I'll do it as soon as you ask me nicely." My eyes flash when they meet hers, and I can see the resolve in her gaze, the tightening of her jaw as my stubborn, sexy as hell wife decides she's going to fight me on this.

Just like I'd hoped.

Overnight Wife

In one smooth motion, I finish undoing the clasp of her jeans and push them down over the arch of her hips. I'm greeted by the sight of bright red panties, silky and thin. It makes me grin.

"Someone was hoping for a naughty encounter when she got dressed this morning," I point out.

Mara's face flushes, almost as red as her panties. "Not necessarily."

I tilt my head, still grinning. "No?" I flatten my hand, slip it underneath her panties. My fingers inch closer and closer to her mound, to the tight little center between her luscious thighs. "So you wear sexy underwear every day then? Good to know..."

"It just helps me feel more confident," she protests. "When I'm... doing something... new." Her breath goes softer, hitching, as my fingertips reach the creases of her thighs. I trace one after the next, digging my finger in, pressing against the soft, sensitive skin there. She's clean-shaven, which only makes my grin wider.

"Something new, hmm?" I arch an eyebrow. "We'll have to get creative then, since we already did so much..."

Her cheeks flare again, but she arches her hips up to meet my hand, too. "That's not what I meant."

"I'm sure." With that, I shift my hand to the side, spreading the lips of her pussy with my index and middle fingers. She gasps, probably thanks to the cool air in the car. I can already tell just from the sensation of pressing my index finger between her lips, that she's drenched. Her juices coat my finger in an instant, even more so when I begin to drag it back and forth along the length of her slit, slow and teasing.

Another moan escapes her throat, this one longer, as I circle her entrance with my fingertip.

"You're so fucking wet, darling." I smirk down at her, lying beneath me on the leather car seat. "It's almost like you're enjoying this."

She bites her lower lip, and that expression alone is enough to send a fresh jolt of rock-hard desire to my dick. "I... might be," she admits, breathy with desire.

I push one finger inside her, hard and fast, all the way up to the knuckle. She groans again, bucking up toward me. "Do you want me right here?" I curl my finger inside her, making sure she can feel every inch of it. The tip of my finger pressing hard against her. Then I draw it out slowly, running the tip of my finger over the sensitive skin of her G-spot.

She gasps this time, twisting under me. "M-maybe."

"You want my cock inside you?"

"Yes," she gasps.

I pull my finger out with a slick, wet sound, and grin down at her. "Then say it," I tell her.

Her lips part with surprise. I just watch her, waiting, as I raise my hand to my mouth and slowly lick my finger, savoring the taste of her, salty and a little sweet, a flavor I could never imagine getting enough of.

Her lower lip quivers as she watches me. I wink and bend down to trail my tongue along her body. Lower and lower, until I'm kneeling beneath her, just below the seat, and my tongue circles her navel, dips into it. I gently drag my teeth along the edge of her stomach, trailing my hot mouth down, until I reach her mound, my tongue pressing against her sensitive, smooth skin.

Then I dip between her thighs, pushing them apart just wide enough to press my face between them, my stubble grazing the sensitive skin along her inner thighs on either side of my face, until my tongue reaches her pussy lips. I

Overnight Wife

trace along them, only on the outside, not delving inside her yet.

She quivers, her hands sliding down to run through my hair, and then fisting in my hair. "I..."

"Yes?" I arch an eyebrow, sitting back to gaze up at her, over the plane of her body. I love this view. I love everything about my sexy wife.

I just need her to come around to admitting that she's mine.

Her throat works with a tight swallow, but I can tell from the spark in her eyes that she's still trying to hold out on me. "That feels so good," she murmurs, instead of what I want.

So I decide it's time to play harder.

I spread her lips with my fingertips and trace my tongue along her slit, back to front, then back again. I let the very tip of my tongue graze her clit, just lightly, just enough of a touch to make her gasp and jerk against the seat. Then I slide lower again, circling her entrance, lapping up her juices.

Her breath comes harder, faster, and her hands tighten in my hair.

But I'm not giving her what she wants. Not yet.

I run my tongue along her clit once more, and smile to myself at the sound of her desperate moan. Then I keep going, trailing my tongue back up her body, until I sit up and lean over her again, her hands falling away from my head. I lie along her body, the hard press of my cock digging into her and push her hair back from her face.

"Well?"

"You're impossible," she replies, glaring.

"I just know what I want," I answer, and I can see the way the words affect her. The dilation in her eyes, the hitch in her breath.

"Fine," she finally breathes, the word both a moan and a sigh. Her gaze locks on mine, and I focus on her too, my face inches from hers. So close I can taste her breath in the air, as she says it. "I want my *husband* to fuck me," she whispers.

It's the first time she's ever used that word. It's the first time she's called me her husband.

And it is so fucking hot.

"Your wish is my command," I tell her, reaching down to push my own jeans off. She doesn't wait, her hands trailing after mine, and she pushes my boxers down after them, eager.

Her hands wrap around the base of my shaft the moment it springs free from my boxers. She needs both hands to wrap all the way around me, and her eyes widen as she takes me in. She traces the length of me, base to tip, her thumb tracing over the soft spongy tip of my cock, collecting a drop of precum there.

As I watch, she lifts that thumb to her mouth and sucks it between her lips, eyes locked on mine, imitating me, tasting me the way I tasted her.

Fucking hell, it's hot.

"God, my wife is so fucking sexy," I murmur, as I catch her wrist, and raise one of her arms over her head, pinning her against the seat beneath me.

With my other hand, I reach down to spread her curvy, luscious thighs to either side of my waist. I grasp the base of my cock and guide the tip to her pussy lips, tracing her lips with the smooth, velvet tip of my cock, pressing hard enough to let her feel the hard steel beneath.

I dip the tip between her lips, and trace back and forth along her slit, the same way I did with my finger earlier, collecting juices, teasing her, until the tip glistens with her eagerness.

Overnight Wife

Only then do I thrust forward, spearing her in one hard, slow motion, my hips driving down against hers as she bucks up against me, moaning wild and low in her throat. "Fuck," she gasps, as I fill her completely. I can feel her pussy stretching around my cock, tight as a fist around me, so wet it's easy to draw out of her again and thrust back in, slow but steady.

She wraps both legs around my waist, hooked up around me, and I reach down to cup her ass with my free hand, my fingers digging into the soft, pillowy skin of her ass.

"You feel so fucking tight," I murmur, watching her with a smile. "Wife," I add, and her breath hitches. She can claim not to want this marriage all she wants, but I can see in her eyes how hot she finds that word. This whole situation.

Her gaze drifts to mine, locks on. And it stays there as I pull out of her and thrust in again, harder this time, faster.

Soon she's rocking her hips in time with mine, thrusting up to meet me every time I drive into her, her breaths coming in short, fast little gasps as we start to move harder, faster.

"Fuck yes," she breathes. "Fuck me."

I still inside her then, and arch an eyebrow, eyes on hers. "What was that?" I ask. It takes her a second to realize what she said. To figure out what's missing.

Her whole face burns bright red, but she's too far gone to protest. I can see in her eyes how much she wants this now. "Fuck me, husband," she growls, and that word sends another pulse of desire through me, making this all the hotter as I draw out to thrust inside her again, again.

She's mine, and I intend to keep her. To make sure the whole world knows that she belongs to me, no matter what, from now on.

I angle my hips to make sure my thick cock drags against her inner front wall with every thrust, right along the sweet spot that makes her toes curl and her breath hitch. Watching her come undone beneath me is worth every second of waiting, every moment of teasing and torturing her.

Her lips part, her eyes lock onto mine, and I smile at her, knowing that she's starting to realize it too. "You're mine," I whisper, against her throat, before I kiss and suck gently along the edge of her jawline, making her fists clench, her nails digging harder into my shoulders.

"I'm yours," she breathes, and I can feel her pussy clenching harder around me. This close, she can't hide the way those words turn her on too—it's written all over her face, in her eyes, in her every movement, as she pulls me closer, thrusts her hips up into mine harder.

"Come for me, wife," I tell her, and those big blue eyes of hers widen. I doubt any man has ever given her such a direct command before. But I keep going, keep thrusting into her, and she keeps arching up to meet me, her breath coming harder and faster. "Come, now," I say again, putting force behind it, letting her know I mean business.

And she does. She comes undone beneath me, crying out as the full force of the orgasm hits her, hard enough to make her toes curl and her whole body shake. Her pussy clenches and releases around my hard cock, convulsing in a way that drives me closer to my own edge.

I don't wait for her orgasm to pass. I just keep thrusting into her, again and again, until I can't hold back anymore. With one last hard thrust and a sound that's almost a growl, I finish deep inside her, my hands digging into her soft curves as I pin her against me, pleasure flooding my body, lighting every inch of me on fire.

Overnight Wife   79

But far from feeling satisfied, when we draw apart again, she only leaves me wanting more. I have a feeling that a woman like her always will.

* * *

I drive Mara back to her place, casting sideways glances at her the whole time. "You're quiet," I point out, when we're near the address she gave me to plug into my navigation system.

"Just tired," she says, avoiding my eyes. But I notice out of the corner of my eye the way she keeps stealing glances at me, probably when she thinks I'm too busy paying attention to the road to notice her.

She underestimates my ability to multitask. Or maybe she just underestimates how much I notice about her—how everything she does catches my eye, draws my attention. I couldn't have chosen a better wife for myself if I'd been trying to do it on purpose.

That thought sets off a memory. An unpleasant clench in my stomach. But I push it aside, drive it from my head. There will be time to dwell on all of that when she's not here. When I don't have more important things—a more important *person*—to focus on instead.

I reach across the gear shift to rest my hand on her knee. She leans toward my touch, an unconscious reaction, before she seems to catch herself, and freezes in place. "Relax," I tell her with a grin. "You can let yourself enjoy this, you know."

She starts to laugh before she catches herself and clamps her lips together. She inhales, like she's going to say something, but after a pause, she just shakes her head. "I had fun tonight," she says. "A lot of fun."

"I know." My smile widens.

She rolls her eyes, but she smiles, too. "I just... I don't know if I want this yet, John. I'm not sure it's a good idea."

"I am," I tell her. "And I'm never wrong."

She sighs, but she reaches down to twine her fingers through mine at the same time. "For some insane reason, I'm starting to hope you might be right," she admits, her voice soft and low.

We pull up outside her house, and I lean over to cup her chin, tilting her face toward mine and pulling her into a long, slow, searing kiss. She melts against me, her eyes fluttering shut. But I don't close mine. I keep them focused on her. On my goal.

I know what I want, after all. And I'm good at getting it.

We draw apart, just as my phone starts to buzz. She glances at it, but it's facedown, so she can't see whose name is on the screen. "Do you want to get that?" she asks.

I shake my head. "Later." Then I draw her back to me, kiss her again, her lips parting beneath mine, melting. I lose track of time, of anything but the taste of her, the scent of her, the feel of her in my arms.

My hands slide down over her curves, toward her belly, past it. I pause at the hem of her jeans, and I feel her arch up against me, feel her starting to breathe harder in anticipation. But before things get too hot and heavy again, I draw back and flash her a sly grin.

"Think of me tonight when you're touching yourself," I tell her. "Tomorrow, I'll want details."

Her cheeks flush, but she doesn't protest. Then I kiss her once more and hit the button to open her door. "Goodnight, John," she says, her voice hitching on that last word.

"Sleep well, wife." I have time to catch the tail end of her smile, before she turns toward her house. I watch to make

Overnight Wife   81

sure she gets inside safely. Before she closes the door behind herself, I notice her check back over her shoulder, looking at me one last time.

That only makes my smile widen. I know she's into this. She may not know it yet, but she wants this marriage every bit as much as I do.

If perhaps not for exactly the same reasons.

My phone starts to buzz again, and I frown, shutting my eyes and pinching the bridge of my nose for a moment. I ignore the call, letting it go to voicemail, preferring to text rather than talk. *I did what you wanted. I'll bring her to meet you next weekend.*

The moment it finishes sending, I shut my phone off, unwilling to deal with the inevitable fallout that will no doubt cause. Then I heave another deep sigh as I pull away from the curb, Mara's house vanishing in my rearview mirror, and wonder if I'm doing the right thing.

8

MARA

After a week of working together, I'm still not sure how I feel about... well, *any* of this. But I love my work, and I've been really enjoying getting my hands dirty in the shop every day. Not to mention, training Daniel has been fun—he's a fast learner, and ever since his first mishap with the machinery, he's been good about asking me for help when he tries out any of the machines for the first time.

I can't deny that it's been nice to get to know John better, too. Most nights of the week, I stay late, and he stays in his own office until the whole place clears out. Only when there's nobody else in the building—per my request, since the last thing I want people thinking is that I'm just some bimbo who slept her way into a job—does he come and find me, usually working next to me at the bench until I'm satisfied my work is done for the evening.

Sometimes we do other things on the bench, after the work is finished. More reasons I don't want any of our coworkers to know the exact nature of our relationship.

But I still haven't taken the ring off. And neither has he, I've noticed.

It's raised more than a few eyebrows around the office. But at least I haven't seen any media leaks about it yet. We seem to have lucked out in terms of avoiding the paparazzi's attention. Part of me knows it's only a matter of time before someone sees us together or notices John's ring finger and starts to ask questions.

But for the moment, I'm just trying to do what John suggested after that first night out together—our first date, kind of. *You can let yourself enjoy this*. And I've been trying to.

The sex, at least, has been off the fucking charts. He seems to know my body even better than I know it myself. He's able to draw out my desire, taunt and tease me until I'm practically screaming to come, and when he finally gives me that release, it's like nothing I've ever experienced before.

Last night, for example, bent over the workbench where I'm working dutifully now... The memories are hot enough to make my face flush.

"Is it too hot in here?" Daniel calls across the room, making me blush again for an entirely different reason. "I can turn the air up."

"I'm fine, thanks," I mumble, and turn back to my work, trying my best to stay focused on it, and not on memories of how good it felt when John knelt at the edge of the table and ran his tongue up my inner thighs, one after the next, teasing, tasting, until his tongue finally reached my pussy lips, parted and explored them slowly, until I was gasping so loudly I'm surprised the night security guard didn't hear.

Clearly focusing is not working well today.

My phone buzzes, and I glance at it, then startle out of my seat. It's an unknown number, but the area code is Las Vegas.

I've been calling and leaving voicemails at the Vegas town

Overnight Wife

hall for days, after my online research into how to annul a marriage proved worthless. Everything I read told me I'd need to go back there in person, which is out of the question, at least for now. I'm too busy trying to get this big project for Pitfire out the door—it's the first one they've entrusted to me. The last thing I want to do this early on is look like a flake or ask for time off—especially if I'd be taking that time off because I accidentally eloped with the CEO.

But maybe there's a way to have this marriage annulled by mail. It won't hurt to call them back.

I excuse myself and step out into the stairwell, which I've already learned is soundproof through some seriously thorough research with John, late on Wednesday night, him pinning me against the wall. Once the door shuts after me, I dial back the number, holding my breath.

"Las Vegas town hall, Valerie speaking," answers a prim voice on the other end, and my stomach plummets.

"Hi, this is Mrs. Walloway," I say. "I left some voicemails—"

"About the annulment process, yes. It's quite simple, ma'am, I understand not everyone can file in person. There's a form on our website you can print out..."

I scramble in my pocket for a piece of scrap paper and a pen to jot down notes about what she's saying. I write down the website address, the specific form, but then her voice makes me hesitate.

"You'll just need to mail it in to us within the next two weeks, during the the grace period for a simplified annulment. After that, I'm afraid things will get a little bit more complicated."

I bite the inside of my cheek. *Two weeks.* My stomach flips again, much less settled than it was earlier today.

Before I knew there was a ticking clock over my head. A timeline to decide...

What? There's no decision to be made here, not really. We made a mistake, and we need to fix it.

But part of me isn't so sure anymore. Part of me can't stop thinking about how good it feels when we're together. When John has his hands all over me, his mouth on my body, his cock inside me. My cheeks flush with heat, as the lady on the other end of the phone continues to explain the process. I'm only half listening.

The rest of me is wondering if I'm starting to lose my mind, or if this really is starting to sound like a possibility.

By the time I hang up the phone, I have to lean against the wall and take some deep breaths before I can go back into the workshop and pretending everything is normal.

My phone buzzes again, startling me so badly I almost drop it. But when I check the screen, I see it's just Lea. *Lunch?*

I text her back right away. *Yes please.* What I really need now is to talk this over with a neutral party. A friend who was there and knows exactly how this situation got so wild in the first place. She'll talk sense into me. She'll explain that it's been fun to enjoy my time with John, but that I can't go and stay married, let alone to my boss, and potentially blow up my first job in the industry.

I need to get my priorities back in order, and my best friend is just the person to help me do that. Even if she can be a bad influence on nights out, when push comes to shove, Lea's always practical where it really counts.

With a fresh distraction in my immediate future, I push my way back into the studio, intent on grabbing my things and heading straight to lunch. I don't make it farther than

Overnight Wife 87

my desk, though, before a familiar face appears beside it, wearing a bright, curious smile.

"Mara! Hadn't seen you this morning. I was wondering if you were in yet." Bianca grins and offers me a coffee.

Bianca has been great this week too. Almost as friendly and easygoing as Daniel. Not to mention, her habit of providing caffeine for all the staff, no matter the hour of the day, has certainly saved my sanity more than once when my energy is flagging.

"Thank you." I accept the coffee, my second of the day, and raise it toward her in a toast. "But yeah, got here early as usual."

"You were here so late last night too, though, weren't you?" she asks.

"No rest for the wicked," I joke, taking a sip of the coffee. Two creamers, just the way I like it. Bianca's got a good head on her shoulders. She notices a lot more than people give her credit for, I've realized. It wouldn't surprise me if she works her way up the corporate ladder quickly. I'm surprised she went in for a secretarial job at all, considering she seems more the business major and marketing type.

Then again, she is always talking about how much she admires John, and how much she wants to learn from him. She keeps calling him a genius, too. Often enough that I worry his ego might grow out of control if he listens to her for too long.

"What time did you finally get home?" Bianca looks worried, concerned about my sleep schedule—or lack thereof—maybe.

I blush again, remembering what I was distracted by most of the second half of the evening. "Oh, I don't know, eleven maybe?"

"John stayed late too, didn't he?" She cocks her head,

looking so innocently curious that it just makes my flush even more obvious.

I force my smile to remain steady, and clench my hands a little harder around the hot coffee cup. "I guess so," I reply, my smile turning forced. "Excuse me for the moment, though, Bianca. I was just about to head out for lunch."

"Oh!" Her eyes shift to my hand. My left hand, I notice. Then they dart away again. "Are you meeting someone? Your husband?"

"Just a friend," I answer, and this time I really do manage to extract myself, grabbing my purse from the desk and bringing the coffee with me as I beeline toward the exit.

That was close. Too close. The hairs on the back of my neck are still standing on end, my stomach churning with worry. *Does she suspect something? Has she noticed that both John and I have been staying late every night this week?*

Moreover, would she tell anyone else, if she did notice?

I force myself to forget about it for now. There's nothing I can do in the meantime. And who knows, maybe this will all be a moot point soon anyway.

That's what I need to decide now, after all.

I spend most of the drive to the restaurant going through the two competing scenarios. In one, John and I annul this marriage and continue as coworkers. And I spend every day for the next however long I'm at this company trying to forget about how it felt to be with him. Trying to forget the mind-blowing orgasms, or how hot it is to hear him call me his wife as we fuck. Trying not to think about the searing hot glances he shoots my way when nobody else is looking, glances that promise just how many filthy things he's doing to me in his head.

Forget undressing me with his eyes. John full on fucks me with his.

Overnight Wife   89

And then there's all our late-night talks over the work bench about our career goals, the plans we have for our futures. We're surprisingly in sync, on so many things...

Stop it, I tell myself as I pull up to the restaurant. *You can't do this for real.*

But my mind won't stop playing over the other scenario. In that second one, John and I stay married. We tell people, we stop hiding and slinking around in dark corners of restaurants with discrete owners. The whole world finds out that I'm married to one of the richest, most eligible bachelors out there...

And I get to keep him. I get to keep both my job and this man. Maybe my coworkers judge me for it; maybe Daniel and Bianca won't treat me the same way anymore, but is that a good enough reason to give up on something that could be real? Just because people might not understand or approve?

I'm torn up all over again as I stride into the restaurant and pick out Lea along the back wall, already eating an appetizer. That girl could eat most men twice her size under the table. I join her with a hug and steal one of her croquettes. "I finally heard back from Vegas," I say by way of greeting.

"And?" Lea's eyebrows shoot upward. I've kept her filled in on my progress with the annulment so far—or rather, the lack thereof until today. But I haven't told her everything.

I haven't kept her posted on what's been happening between John and me, exactly.

"I can annul it, but I'd need to do it within the next two weeks in order to do it the easy way."

"Okay. Easy way sounds good." She picks up another croquette and bites in with enthusiasm. "Why do you look so upset, then?"

I bite the inside of my cheek, wondering how much to

tell her. But she's my best friend. And besides, I don't think John would be upset if I said something about us. Far from it —he wants to declare I'm his to the entire world, as he keeps saying. It's taken all my powers of persuasion to keep him from revealing this marriage publicly just yet.

So in the end, I cave. "John and I have been hooking up," I tell her. Then I shake my head. "No, not hooking up; not even fucking. Well... sometimes fucking." She laughs, and my face heats up. "I just... I think maybe it could be something real. I actually like him."

"Mara." She fixes me with a narrowed glare. "You know I love a good wild fling as much as the next girl. And I fully approved of you letting loose for once in Vegas. But you cannot *marry* a guy you barely know. Not yet, anyway! If this becomes a relationship, cool, but date him and think about it for a while, y'know?"

"No, you're right. I know. I just... He's really into this. He *wants* me to be his wife."

Her eyebrows shoot upward. "Okay, first of all, congrats on snagging the world's most eligible bachelor so quickly. But secondly, this is still pretty worrying, don't you think?" She tilts her head. "I mean, what's his motivation? He never seemed like the type to be all traditional about marriage and commitment before... Although, he did have that failed engagement," she muses.

I frown. "He had a what?"

Lea rolls her eyes. "Girl, did you not even google the mega-famous guy you're wedded to?" She reaches for her phone, and a few taps later, I'm staring at an article about John Walloway's "disastrous almost-marriage." It's dated months before we met, but still, it makes something clench in my gut, uncertainty settling in.

Am I just a rebound for him?

I stare at the girl in the grainy photo who's throwing a suitcase full of clothes into the trunk of her car, a trail of clothing behind her leading back into the front of an expensive-looking apartment complex. I bite my lower lip. He never mentioned anything about her.

Then again, neither of us really mentioned anything about our pasts. We were too focused on the present—and in my case on the looming future ahead of us. A future we need to annul before it becomes permanent, and far too real.

"You're right," I murmur. "I'll get the annulment." But deep down, part of me wonders if I actually want it. After all, why does my chest hurt so much just saying those words? And why does it make my head throb, to think about leaving him?

I push the questions away, along with the remaining salad on my lunch plate. My appetite is long gone. "What about you, how are you doing?" I ask Lea, mostly for the distraction. But my head is pounding so much it's hard to even pay attention to her answers.

What am I doing? I just keep asking myself, over and over again.

Back in the office, Daniel catches me staring into space beside the drill machine, my gaze focused on the wall and not on the stack of wood I should be cutting, dremmeling and preparing for assembly. "Penny for your thoughts?" he asks, with a smirk that makes me wonder how much he's guessed about my moodiness lately.

But that's just my paranoia talking. Nobody knows anything. Not about John and me, anyway. Maybe Daniel thinks I'm pining over my mystery husband—a husband I had to lie about because I couldn't get that damn ring off my finger. Now, it's loosened a little, but I still haven't removed it.

I have to wonder what that says about my current mental state.

I tell myself it's just because people at work would start asking too many questions if I suddenly removed the ring now. But deep down, I'm not sure. Deep down, I wonder if there's a subconscious reason I keep this on. Or if maybe it's just for the flash of desire I spot in John's eyes every time he sees me, checks for the ring, and finds it still on my finger.

Part of me doesn't want to let him go this easily, despite this mess.

So I force a smile at Daniel and I lie. "Just tired," I say. "Long night last night."

"You were here late, weren't you?"

Man, does everyone in this company keep obsessive track of one another's schedules? Still, I shrug and nod, because it's true. I was here late. And most of the time I spent working.

A little bit of it I spent doing other things, but hey...

Daniel claps me on the shoulder, squeezing just once, but enough to reassure me that he doesn't suspect anything. "Take it easy," he says. "You don't want to burn out after your first week here, after all, right?"

"You're right," I tell him, forcing a smile.

"Mara?" Bianca's voice catches me off-guard. I turn and find her leaning against the doorway of the shop, arms crossed. "Mr. Walloway sent for you. He wants to talk in his office."

"Oh, of course," I reply, trying to defuse the sudden bright red flush that creeps over my cheeks, the pulse of

Overnight Wife   93

desire that flares through my veins at the thought of what John might want in his office. Of what he might want to do to me right now.

It's work, I tell myself. *And it's the middle of the day. He probably just wants normal, work-related things.*

"I'll be right there," I add, because Bianca is squinting at me, in what I hope I'm just imagining seems like a suspicious way. She flashes me a smile, and nods, reassuring me that any suspicion is just in my imagination.

You really do need to get more sleep, Mara, I tell myself as I wave a quick goodbye to Daniel and hand over responsibility for the drill machine to him temporarily. *You're making yourself crazy.*

But when I reach the John's office and tap tentatively on the doorframe, I'm reminded that it's not me who's making me crazy. Not entirely.

It's him.

He's dressed, as usual, in a perfectly fitted suit. He has the top button undone, and the casual glance he flashes in my direction when I enter the office quickly shifts into a heated one, his gaze catching fire as it sweeps over my body, lingering on my chest, my hips, my legs, in a way that tells me without any need for words exactly what he's thinking. Exactly how much he wants to grab me and strip me down right here and now.

"Mara," he says, and just that, just my name on his lips, is enough to melt a sweet spot between my thighs, get me wet and hungry and wanting.

I shut the door behind me, before he even needs to ask.

He doesn't wait for more of a response. He crosses his office in two strides and catches me around the waist, pinning me against the door with an audible *thud* before his hands wrap around my neck, cupping my chin and drawing me up into a deep, slow, hard kiss.

When we break apart, it's all I can do to stay on my feet and breathing. But I manage, with only the faintest hitch in my breath, and it makes me proud to know I can withstand this kind of temptation and torture in the middle of the workday.

"Was that all you wanted to talk to me about?" I ask with an arched eyebrow, suppressing a smile.

John's gaze sharpens. "I want you to come away with me this weekend."

I tilt my head. "Where?"

"Not far. Just a little ways outside of town."

My stomach flips. Does he want to take me on a trip? Some kind of vacation? I press my lips together, uncertain, but he anticipates my next question.

"It won't interfere with any of your work, I promise."

We have the same priorities, John and me. I appreciate it more than I expected to. "Okay," I say, not even sure what I've just agreed to. But just that one word lights up his face so much that I know I can't take it back, even if I find out he's dragging me to some kind of horrible and boring event.

Although it's hard to imagine any event being horrible or boring if I'm on John's arm... Or able to sneak away with John for some private time together. Even the dullest classical concert would be incredible if I could distract myself by sliding into his lap in the darkened concert hall, or feel his hands run up my thighs and slip under my skirt...

As if he's reading my mind, John catches my me again and pins me against the door, his lips finding mine a second time. I part my lips beneath his, let his tongue slip in, exploring my mouth, claiming me. At the same time, his hands roam further down, gripping my waist, pulling

Overnight Wife

me against him so tightly that I can feel him starting to harden against me, his cock pressed right against my belly, so thick I can feel him even through the fabric of both our pants.

"We can't," I whisper when we break apart. "Not here."

"I know." His eyes flash, and there's more in them than just desire and excitement. Something I can't put my finger on.... "After this weekend," he murmurs, "everything will change."

My stomach flips again, though I don't even know what he means. Are we going to annul this after all? Are we going back to Vegas to fix our mistakes? Or is it something else?

"John..." I don't know what I want to ask. *Where are we really going this weekend?* That seems like a question he'll refuse to answer. Or maybe just *What's on your mind?*

Before I can put words to it, though, he silences me again with another kiss, hard and fast, before he almost pushes me away from him, my body tilting back into the door with the force of it.

"Go," he says. "Get back to work. We need to work overtime if we want to take the whole weekend off."

I frown, confused by the sudden shift. But I listen to him anyway, backing away slowly, waiting until he's back at his desk, arms crossed on top of it, before I risk opening the office door again, running a hand through my hair at the same time and hoping it's not mussed from our kiss, from his hands running through my hair and cupping my body against him.

All I want to do is slam the office door shut and lock it behind me. Slide under his desk of his and go down on him, tracing my tongue along the length of his hard cock over and over, sucking him into my mouth until he gives in and tells me what's going on. Until he tells me where he's taking me this weekend and why the idea of it has him so keyed up —acting so hot one second and cold the next.

But I can't do that. Not here. Not while everyone else we work with is still in the office, and while I have Lea's warning fresh in my mind—plus that memory of John's ex with all her things flung everywhere, leaving in a car... I need to be clearing my head of him, not clouding it further.

So I open the office door and slip out without another word, closing it tightly behind me.

I don't make it more than a few steps from the entrance before I spot Bianca across the office floor. Her eyes catch mine—was she staring? Watching the office, listening to us in there? My stomach clenches all over again, for a different reason this time.

But then she flashes a sweet smile and turns back to her own desk, and I shake my head. I'm just being paranoid. Imagining things. That's all this is.

The only people in this office thinking constantly about John and me are the two of us. So I smile back and retreat to the workroom, shoulders squared, head up. Whatever's going on between us, maybe this weekend will bring more clarity.

And if not? Well, then I'll still have enough time to make the annulment deadline afterward. I try to ignore the heavy knot in my gut at the thought of that. *It's for the best,* I tell myself. *Lea is right.*

I need to be practical about this.

9
___

JOHN

Today is the day. I stare at myself in the rearview mirror of my car, waiting. I haven't hit send on the text to let Mara know that I'm parked outside. I needed a minute to myself. A minute to wrap my head around what I'm about to do.

If I do this... if I take her with me today... Everything will change. And who knows how she'll feel by the end of this, or what she'll decide to do.

But it has to happen. I need to do this.

So why do I still feel so guilty about it?

Because this is the wrong way to do this, whispers a little voice at the back of my mind. A voice I ignore, as I hit send on the text I've already written. *I'm outside, Mara.* I didn't tell her anything about this weekend—I didn't want to scare her off, or worse, make her feel sorry for me. But I did let her know to pack for warm weather, and the moment she steps out of the lobby of her apartment building, I see that she's done just that.

It takes all of my self-control to stay seated in the car and not jump out to grab her right away. Because she looks *incredible.* Every step she takes makes the blue flowing skater-dress she's wearing flow around her calves, each swish flashing just a hint of thigh that only makes me want more.

It's more dressed up than I've ever seen my jeans-and-T-shirts girl, and it makes me want to tear that dress right off of her. She climbs into the passenger seat with a smile and a wave, and before she can get a word out, I catch her around the waist and drag her toward me, kissing her cheek, her jawline, her neck.

"You look incredible," I murmur against her skin, feathering her with kisses, dipping lower, toward the neckline of the dress, low enough to reveal just a hint of cleavage—enough to let me know I want more.

She laughs and twines her arms around me, her fingers tracing through my hair. "If I'd known this would be your reaction, I'd wear dresses more often."

"You should," I tell her, my hands sliding down her hips, marveling at the smoothness of her curves beneath the stretch of cottony fabric. My hands reach the hemline of the dress, touch bare skin, and start to inch higher, along her thighs.

She squirms a little and glances at the windows of the car. It's broad daylight outside, after all, and we're parked right in front of her house. But I don't care.

"Maybe we should cancel," I tell her, before I lean in to drag my teeth along the edge of her jawline, nipping her skin just roughly enough to make her gasp and arch up against me. "Go back into your apartment and forget the weekend. We'll stay here, eat in..." I lean back to catch her eye with a feral grin. "I've already got plenty to devour right here." My hands skate across her thighs, along the flat of her stomach.

She shivers beneath me, and it's the most delicious feel-

Overnight Wife

ing, knowing how much I affect her. How easily I can turn her on. A breathy little moan escapes her lips as my hand dips lower, grazing along the edge of her panties—I can feel the fabric of them through the dress, and I press a little harder, until her hips arch up against my hand.

But then she stops. Pulls away from me, with what looks like Herculean effort. "We can't bail," she says, though the hitch in her breath and the flush in her cheeks tell me she wants to be saying anything but this. "You said it's important," she adds. "Whatever *it* is."

My stomach clenches, and my throat seals itself up. I clear it with a growl and turn back toward the road, reaching up to grip the wheel with both hands—the only way I can think of to make them stop touching her. "Bailing might be the wiser move," I murmur under my breath.

After all, if we bail now, she'll never need to know. She'll never have to look at me differently—or worse, decide that this is all too much for her. I wouldn't blame her, of course, after this. Who knows how it's going to go? But there's a tiny, crazy part of me that hopes she'll stay. Even after she realizes what she's in for.

"John?" Her hand comes to rest on my wrist, soft and delicate.

I turn my hand around to thread my fingers through hers and bring it up to my lips, kissing each finger, one by one. "Let's go," I say, dropping her hand, and she pulls it back to her lap, wrapping her fist around the hem of her skirt, her eyes on me, curious.

But I shake it off and put the car in drive, ignoring her stares as best I can. At least she knows better than to try to pry more details from me. I appreciate it. At this stage, I'm not sure I could stand talking about this. Showing her is better. Like leaping into the deep end of a pool. There's no time to get cold feet or decide the water's too unfriendly after all and climb back out. This way, once we get started, there'll be no going back.

I floor the accelerator, and Mara changes the topic. She talks about work, about the latest project we've been putting together. I relax a little, settling into the more familiar, easier topic. We bat around set ideas for a particularly important scene of the play we're staging. Mara, as usual, has brilliant ones. And better yet, whenever I pitch ideas, she questions them. Pushes me to make them clearer, smarter, better.

It's just one of the many things I adore about her. She makes me a better version of myself.

So why am I dragging her into this mess? I shake off the doubt as we reach the exit. It's near Palm Springs, though not quite all the way into the desert yet. I take the familiar exit, wind through the all too memory-filled town, taking smaller streets with every turn until I finally turn up one long, winding driveway, through a manicured lawn that speaks to the fact that, despite recent droughts, whoever lives here has the money to keep up appearances.

Mara's gaze on my face sharpens. But when I glance over at her, I can practically see her biting her tongue, resisting the urge to question this.

We reach the end of the drive, and the house towers ahead of us. House is the wrong word, really. Mansion would be more appropriate.

I should know. I bought it for them.

My parents are already waiting out front, arms hooked around one another. The end of the drive is filled with cars. Extended family, friends of the family, distant relatives. My parents love doing this—hosting events, throwing parties. Showing off the property their son earned them.

It was their idea to make this a surprise. When they

Overnight Wife 101

learned about Mara—when they learned that I finally, *finally* settled down, as they've been trying to force me to do for years—they insisted. But now, watching her reaction shift from surprise to confusion to worry, I wonder yet again if this was the right move. If I shouldn't have told her everything, right from the beginning.

"What is this, John?" Mara murmurs as I park right in front of the drive, in the spot of honor. My dad waves, and my mom beams like she's just won some kind of award.

In her mind, she probably has.

"My parents wanted to meet my new wife," I tell her, shutting off the engine. "They insisted on throwing a party. It's not huge; just some friends and family—"

"You didn't warn me I'd be *meeting your parents,*" she hisses under her breath. But there's no time for her to build up steam. The door is already sliding open, and my parents are calling their hellos.

"You must be Mara." My mom reaches her first, before Mara even has time to fully exit the car. She wraps her in a tight bear hug, and then Dad joins in, shaking her hand like she's a business partner, not my wife.

Well. I suppose both terms are accurate, technically.

"We've heard so much about you," Mom is gushing, although that's not strictly accurate. They didn't even know Mara existed until I finally admitted it to them a few days ago. Less than a week.

Mara shoots me a confused look over Mom's shoulder, but she hugs her back, and deals with my dad's hand-pumping decently well.

"Mom." I step over to kiss her cheek. "Give her some breathing room; you're going to suffocate her."

"Of course, of course." Mom backs away, although there's still a hungry glean in her eye as she assesses Mara.

"Come in, darling, have some lunch. You must be famished. Eating for two and all." Mom winks, and I groan under my breath.

Already?

Mara's face flushes, and she frowns, confused. "Er... no, just eating for the one, actually," she says, and it's embarrassingly obvious how quickly my mother's expression deflates with disappointment.

Still, at least she doesn't press the issue, hooking an arm through Mara's and leading her toward the house. I fall into step beside my father and trail after them.

"Your mother's beside herself," he says.

"With happiness or annoyance?" I respond archly.

Dad chuckles. "You know her. Why not both at once?" He shoots me a sideways look. "She's pleased you're finally settling down, of course. But she wanted a big wedding, a splashy engagement party..." Dad gestures at the house. "Hence all of this hoopla, naturally."

"I thought you told me you could tamper her. That this would just be a small get-together." I side-eye the driveway, unable to stop counting. At least a dozen cars, maybe more.

"This *is* small," Dad insists. "You should have seen the original guest list she wanted."

I roll my eyes with a groan, but it's quickly drowned by the roar of our relatives as we enter the house. My cousins swarm, followed by aunts, uncles, friends of my parents. Mara has time to catch my eye just once, panic written all over her face, before she's swallowed in hugs and congratulations.

I watch them watching her. Some of their congratulations are heartfelt, sincere. Others are grasping, reaching. Most of my relatives are decent people, really. But they look at my bank account; they see my name in the newspapers,

Overnight Wife

and they can't help themselves. After all, decent people or not, everyone's attitudes shift when they get close to money. Especially the kind of money I have.

The kind of money that let me buy a house like this for my parents. The kind of money that restored this family name to the prominence it once had, way back when.

I care about my family, of course. But you can't choose your family. And mine, well... they can be more of a handful than most.

I weave through a sea of aunts to reach Mara, and loop an arm around her waist, feeling how tense every muscle in her body is. She tilts her head back to rest against my shoulder, in a move that raises a sea of *awws* from the surrounding family members. But when she leans in to whisper in my ear, it's not the sort of sweet-nothing I'm sure they imagine she's saying.

"What the hell did you just throw me into?" she whispers.

I lean down to kiss her jawline, right where it reaches the lobe of her ear. My tongue darts across her diamond earring, toying with it, making a little sigh escape her lips before I respond. "My parents wanted it to be a surprise," I murmur, my breath ghosting across her cheek, drawing a little shiver from her. "My mother insisted that I owed her. I believe the words were 'you robbed me of a wedding.'"

Mara tilts her head back far enough to catch my eye, steel glinting in hers. "Still. You should have at least warned me. There are so many people here—"

"They don't matter." I turn her to face me, cupping her face between my palms. "Nobody matters but you and me, Mara."

Her breath catches in her throat. Her pupils dilate where they fix on mine. "John..."

"John." My mother's voice breaks through our conversation, as her hand comes to rest on my shoulder. "Don't monopolize your beautiful bride," she says, teeth flashing in a wide smile. "After all, you've had her to yourself for weeks. We want to get to know her."

With an eye roll just for Mara, I shift a little, letting my mother hook an arm through Mara's.

"Come on, dear, you haven't even seen the gift table yet. It was tricky to figure out a good gift, of course—John here wouldn't give us any hints about your tastes. I hope it's all right—we decided it would be safer to just buy for the future instead…"

I trail after my mother, who's leading Mara toward an elaborate table set up near the rear wall. There are a few gift-wrapped boxes on it, some cards, and… *Oh God.* My stomach sinks.

A bassinet.

Is she crazy?

"Mother," I say, raising my voice.

Mom doesn't stop. "We figured you'd need all of this soon," my mother babbles, pointing at the blatant baby supplies. There are bottles, little onesies, even a car seat.

Mara tugs her arm from my mother's with force. "Mrs. Walloway, this is all so sweet, but it's… it's too much." Her face is flushed, and I can tell she's trying not to panic.

I understand. So am I. I knew my parents wanted children, for me to carry on the lineage, but this is too far, even for them.

"Nonsense dear. It's never too soon to start planning for the eventual future."

"Eventual…" Mara's face blanches now. "That's a bit presumptuous, don't you think?"

Over Mara's shoulder, my mother frowns. "What could

Overnight Wife   105

be presumptuous about carrying on the family? What could be more important than that?"

"My career, for one thing," Mara counters.

My mother's frown deepens. We're attracting attention now—a couple of cousins have noticed us and are exchanging sideways smirks. It makes me want to grab Mara and pull her out of here right now. I knew this party would be leaping into the deep end, but I didn't think it would end in us drowning. "Career is one thing, but family must come first, dear."

"Oh really?" Mara arches an eyebrow. "Why, because I'm young and female, I must want to pop out a baby immediately?"

"Nobody said anything about immediately, but don't be naïve. Our family needs an heir. John needs children, to carry on our name, our legacy."

"He *needs* them?" Mara shoots me a glare over her shoulder. "That's news to me. He hasn't mentioned wanting anything of the sort."

"Well, I would have thought that would be implied," my mother responds, nonplussed. "After all, he keeps you well, doesn't he? All that money and privilege doesn't come free, dear."

Mara's gaze narrows where it's fixed on mine. "Oh, so I'm being paid to be a baby incubator, is that it?" When she speaks, it's not directed at my mother anymore, but right at me. "Forget it. The last thing I need is to be some kind of kept woman." She shoves away from my mother, straight through the gaggle of cousins.

Away from me.

I flash one last glare at my mother, who spreads her hands wide, an innocent look on her face, like she doesn't know what she just did. "Thank you for that," I mutter, and then I beeline after Mara.

Forget the rest of them. They don't matter. Only she does.

People are whispering now, pointing. Most are thankfully too distracted eating and drinking their fill. Wringing every last drop of free anything they can from this party.

Screw them all.

This was a mistake, whispers that little voice ins my head, louder now, more insistent. I try to ignore it, scanning the party for Mara. But she's not in the living room or the dining room anymore. The gift table sits ignored, the presents unopened.

I finally find her in the backyard. There's a big tree, one of the few that survived the droughts, with a patch of scrub grass under it. Mara's sitting cross-legged there, facing away from the house, face buried in both hands.

I step up behind her, hesitate for a second, and then kneel next to her. "I'm sorry," I say.

"How could you do this to me?" She looks up at me, her jaw clenched, wiping harder at the tears that keep falling.

"I didn't know she would lay into you like that," I murmur. "I knew my mother wanted me to have kids, but... I didn't think she'd be *this* insane about it."

Mara's throat works with a tight swallow. "You can't just drop shit like this on me without warning, John. Your parents honestly think I'm some kind of—"

"Fuck what they think," I interrupt. "You and I both know why we got married. It doesn't matter what anyone else expects from this marriage. Only what we do."

"Yeah?" Mara lifts her face, jaw set tightly. "Well, after this, I'm starting to think *I* want that annulment."

My stomach sinks. My eyebrows shoot upward. "Mara—"

"No. You keep insisting this is a real marriage, or at least that you want it to be. But no real marriage would have situations like this." She flings a hand behind her, toward the house. "In a real marriage, you'd communicate with me. You'd have told me about your family. Hell, in a real marriage, I'd have had a few years to get used to your baby-crazy parents before I had to meet them for the first time, with them acting like I'm some gold-digger you married off the street."

"Do not call yourself that," I reply, the words harsher than I mean them.

She shoves to her feet. "Why not? It's what everyone thinks, isn't it? That, or they think you knocked me up and we got married in some kind of shotgun wedding." She tugs at the ring on her left finger. "What's everyone going to think when this gets out into the media?" She gestures at the house. "You really think every single person in there is going to keep your new marriage a secret?"

"They know better than to discuss my business with paparazzi—"

"So you think." She shakes her head, scowling. "This was a bad idea. All of it. I should have gotten this marriage annulled the moment I woke up in Vegas. Pretending we had any other options, that was a mistake."

"Mara, don't just give up on this."

"Give up on what? We've known each other for a couple of weeks. You'll be over me in no time." She sets her jaw hard.

I stand next to her, reach for her. But she pulls away. "I'm not giving up on you," I say.

"You should," she replies. "Clearly I'm not the right

woman for you. You should marry someone who wants kids and a family, the white picket fence life."

"Why? I don't want that," I reply.

"You don't want kids?" She raises an eyebrow, doubt written all over her face.

"I do someday, but not right now, not if it will stand in the way of your career—of either of our careers."

But she's shaking her head, already reaching into a hidden pocket of her dress to produce her phone. "Find yourself another baby mama, John, because it's not me." She taps on the screen. "I'm taking an Uber home."

"Let me drive you." But she's already walking away.

"Don't follow me," she says, as if she's reading my mind. Because that's exactly what I want to do. Chase her until she sees that this is the wrong move. *Make* her understand. We belong together.

She stops and turns to me, and I hold my breath because I think maybe she's changed her mind. "If you value me at all, John, give me space right now," she says.

Hope dashed, but what can I do?

I stand there, fists balled at my sides, and watch her walk away. Just like she asked. Even if it's the last thing in the world I want to do.

10
―――

MARA

Called it, I think miserably, rolling over in bed, the article open on my phone screen. Lea texted it to me first thing this morning. It's all over the gossip rags. Big splashy headlines about John Walloway's mysterious new wife.

There's even a photo. Grainy, taken at a distance, of me and John underneath the tree in his parents' backyard. It's far enough away that you can't tell that we're arguing with our heads bent together.

But you can tell it's me, if you've met me. There's no way everyone at work won't see this and know who I'm married to now. Know about John and me, everything.

God damn it. I knew someone in that shady family of his would spill this secret.

I shut my eyes, and behind my eyelids, all I can see is his mother's face again. That deceptively sweet smile on her face, as she says *All that money and privilege doesn't come free, dear.* My stomach churns. *He keeps you well, doesn't he?*

Fuck that. Fuck being a kept woman. Fuck whatever everyone at work will think too—probably that I slept my way into the job, or that John only hired me because he wanted to marry me.

I roll back over in bed with another groan. But sleep is going to be impossible now. So I roll out of bed and get dressed, even though it's going to make me almost an hour early for work. But better that than just lying here staring at my ceiling. Better to get my hands dirty, to keep them occupied in something, anything, other than wallowing.

When I get to the office, it's empty. Which suits me just fine. I swipe into the work room and get down to business, putting together the display we'd talked about on the way to John's disastrous family party yesterday. If nothing else, at least his creative ideas are good. Talking to him about work always inspires me. Pushes my ideas to new limits, and makes me come up with newer, more creative suggestions than I ever would have thought of on my own.

If only working together were our only concern.

I bend over the power tools, letting the drilling sound drown out any other thoughts. I try to force regret and fear from my mind. I try not to think about those stupid gossip articles, and what it's going to mean for my life now that I'm married to the most eligible bachelor in LA, and especially in my industry.

For some reason, it doesn't help as much as I think it will, this burying myself in work thing. But it at least distracts me for a minute.

Then the hour is up, and the rest of my coworkers start flooding into the office, and any illusion of distraction or safety I might have built up for myself falls away.

Daniel's the first one through the doors. The look he shoots me tells me immediately that he knows. His brow is furrowed, and when I call out a hello, he just nods, not saying anything, barely even really acknowledging me. He

Overnight Wife

looks embarrassed, but he slides past me and heads to his own machine.

My stomach clenches. If even *Daniel* is going to judge me for this...

It's a slow processing of that. One by one, my employees file in, and when I give them assignments or ask them about what they're planning to work on today, they just mumble one word answers and avoid eye contact, whereas before they were all eager to talk to me and exchange ideas.

Only Bianca is different.

She flounces in with two cups of coffee, just like every morning, and brings me mine, prepared just the way I like it. Before I can say a word, she reaches out to squeeze my shoulder. "Don't worry," she says. "People will get used to this in time. Just give them a minute to adjust."

It feels like a stone dropped into the pit of my stomach. "You heard," I say. It's not a question.

She grimaces in sympathy. "I'm pretty sure everyone has google alerts set to the boss's name, so yeah. We've all heard." Her gaze drifts toward the ring on my finger.

I'd forgotten I was still wearing it, until just this moment. It had become so second nature, an extension of my hand, but now my finger itches, and I fight the urge to tear it off me. I swallow hard and settle for twisting it around so the diamond faces my palm instead. Less obvious, or at least so it feels. "It's not what it looks like," I say. But how can I explain? *I didn't know who he was when I eloped with him?* That makes it sound even worse than marrying your boss, sleeping your way into a job.

"I don't blame you if it is," Bianca says softly, her voice low enough that none of the rest of our coworkers will be able to hear her. "This industry is near impossible to get a leg up in. It's smart to use every advantage you can to get ahead. I'd never blame a woman for using every weapon at her disposal."

Advantage. Weapon. Like this is all some kind of war or game that I'm fighting. Not just a drunken night out, a stupid mistake that I should have corrected a long time ago. "I didn't marry him for the job," I say, truthfully. "He hired me long before there was anything between us. Honestly, if I'd known how all this looked, I never would have married him in the first place," I add in a lower voice.

Bianca's forehead puckers with concern. "You regret it?"

"I regret how it looks," I respond. "Everyone thinks I slept my way into this job, don't they? They'll never respect me. Not the way they used to. Or were starting to, anyway."

"Well…" Bianca bites her lower lip, looking thoughtful. "You could fix that."

"How?" I ask, shaking my head. "The damage is done."

"Not necessarily…" Bianca studies me. Then she shakes her head. "But I shouldn't interfere—"

"Please," I interrupt. "Any tips are appreciated."

"Well." She surveys the room again. I follow her gaze and know exactly what she's seeing. All our coworkers— people who up until yesterday respected me. Viewed me as a leader, someone whose ideas and orders they respected. "You could always end the marriage. I mean, if you regret it, and if you're already thinking about how much it's changed…"

I wince. "Honestly? I've thought about it. I could annul it, if I act within the next week. There's still time."

"Well, John has experience there, he probably wouldn't care." Bianca purses her lips.

I blink in surprise. "What do you mean?"

She lifts an eyebrow at me, confused. "What, you never even googled your husband?"

Belatedly, I remember the article Lea showed me. His ex. But... "He got married before?" I ask. I thought that girl was only his fiancée.

"Does it count, if you annul it straight after?" Bianca shrugs, her gaze dropping to my ring finger again. "Just a thought."

Just the same thought I've been wrestling with, ever since I woke up in John's bed with this ring on my finger. And yet I still haven't walked away. *Why?*

Because I'm too naïve. Just like John's mother said. A little part of me, a part I'm embarrassed to even admit to, kept expecting this to turn into something more. To maybe become real, the way John claims to have wanted all along.

But it was never real. None of it. And to make matters worse, he's done it before. That girl Lea showed me, his ex, she was more than just his fiancée, if Bianca is to be believed —and to be honest, I trust her information on my husband more than I trust my own. Maybe she's right. Maybe I should have obsessively googled him. Maybe it would have given me more of a warning what this marriage would be like. And what I was getting myself into.

Or at least a warning about the fact that I'm not the first girl he's played this game with.

Fuck this.

I shove away from my desk without another word to Bianca. She watches me go, her eyebrows raised, worry and surprise warring on her face.

But she's right. Lea was right too. Everyone sees this situation clearly. Everyone except me.

John is a player, and I'm done with his games.

I track through the office, and ignore the eyes trailing after me. All of my nosy colleagues are peering after me, probably trying to guess what's going on with me, or wondering why I'm headed toward John's office. I don't care. Our secret is out now, so let them whisper. Let them think I'm headed in there to hook up with him. I don't give a damn about my reputation anymore.

Besides, for once, that's not the truth. I'm on an entirely different mission this time.

I fling open his door, only to find him with the phone raised to one ear, clearly in the middle of a call. But he locks eyes with me, taking me in in one look, in that way only he can do, a way that pierces me to the core, makes me feel seen all the way through. *It's a lie,* I tell myself. *All of this has been a lie.*

"I'll call you back," he says into the phone and hangs up without another word. "Mara." His eyes on mine are almost enough to make me crack.

But I ball my fists and stand my ground. "This is a game to you, isn't it?"

A crease appears between his eyebrows. "If you're talking about the news articles, I assure you, I tried to stop them. You were right, someone at the party must have taken our photo—"

"Do you even care how this makes me look?"

"Of course I care." He stands and crosses around his desk, reaching for me.

But I twist out of his reach. "I'm a laughing stock. Everyone here thinks I slept with you to get my job, married my way into it."

"Who cares what other people think?" He shakes his head.

"I do. I care if my coworkers respect me. I care about my career and being with you has done nothing but jeopardize that at every turn. Ironically, since everyone seems to think it improved it," I add with a scowl.

Overnight Wife   115

He reaches for me again, and again I twist away. "Mara, I'm sorry. I know you're still mad about what happened this weekend, and you have every right to be.

"Is this what you did last time?" I ask, and now his expression shifts, from concern to confusion. I shake my head, not falling for it. "I know you've done all this before. Marriage, annulments." I grab the ring on my finger and tug at it. "I bet you thrive off the drama, don't you?"

"That's not it. Let me explain."

"Oh, so *now* you want to tell me everything? Where was this before, when you should've been letting me know what the hell I was getting into?" With an effort, I manage to wrench the ring free. Then I gasp in pain, glancing down to find a long, angry red scrape along my finger. *Dammit.* It must have been swollen from the gloves I was wearing in the workshop earlier this morning. My ring finger throbs, and a streak of blood appears where I scraped the skin raw.

"Stop." John's hand closes over mine. I try to pull away, but he holds on, reaching with his free hand to his desk and pulling out a tissue. He cleans away the blood, and I grit my teeth at the way it stings, my eyes focused on the floor, the ceiling. Anywhere but on his face, and his worried expression.

When he's finished cleaning away the blood, I thrust the ring at him, shoving it against his chest. He reaches up to take it and our fingertips brush. Even now, despite everything, it sends a thrill through me. A shiver that reaches from the nape of my neck all the way down to my toes.

I ignore it.

But as I'm turning to leave, John clears his throat. "This isn't my first marriage, no."

I glance up at him, but his gaze is on the floor, far away. Despite myself, I remain standing where I am. A little part of me—okay, a big part of me—wants to hear this. I want to give him the chance to explain what he should have told me from the start.

"Her name was Heather. We'd been dating for almost a year. I trusted her, liked her. Maybe even loved her, I don't know. I thought I did at the time, but now, looking back, it was all superficial." He shakes his head. "She just seemed so in sync with me. Seemed to like all the same things I did, wanted to do all the same things. But it was an act." His jaw hardens. "All she really wanted was my money. She convinced me to marry her. Elope. Small ceremony, not even our families there. That should have been my first clue. Not even three days later, I caught her opening a new bank account in both of our names. Trying to transfer huge amounts of my savings to her own accounts."

I wince.

"I found out. And I was able to annul the marriage in time. Of course, she responded by going straight to the tabloids with a tell-all sob story about how I cheated on her and broke her heart." He rolls his eyes. "I hope they paid her well for it. It's the last time her name is going to be relevant anywhere."

"How long ago was this?" I murmur.

"Six months." He shrugs. "Long enough to be old news. I didn't think it was worth dredging up again. Especially not when all I want to do is forget about that period of my life. My own parents were furious—they thought I should have stayed with Heather, despite everything she did. They think marriage is for life. But I couldn't stay with someone like that, someone who was only in this for the money. I never wanted to make that mistake again."

I arch an eyebrow, eyes narrowing. "So why did you run

Overnight Wife   117

away with a complete stranger, then? If you didn't want to make the same mistake twice."

"Are you kidding?" His eyebrows shoot higher. "You're the exact opposite of her, Mara. You're everything I never even knew I could find in one woman. You don't care about money; you care about your career, about doing a job right, about all the things a person ought to put first in life. I admire your fire, your creativity, your passion..." He takes a step closer to me, and this time, I can't bring myself to move away from him.

He catches my hand and pulls it to his chest, carefully kissing the back of my hand, making sure not to touch my shallow cut again.

"From the moment I met you, I've been head over heels for you," he says, and those words send a bolt of pleasure through my veins, make my breath hitch in my chest. "I'm sorry I dragged you into all of this. It was selfish, yes. And none of this is your problem to deal with. Not my parents, or their threats—"

"What do you mean, threats?"

John's face flushes with color. His gaze drops to the floor. "They want a grandchild," he says.

"I gathered that much," I mumble.

He shakes his head. "You don't understand. When I started this company, I was so young. I needed a cofounder for loans, to cosign. My father agreed..."

My forehead puckers. "You mean your father owns part of Pitfire?"

He nods. "He's not involved, not really. But, technically, if he pulled out, or sold his shares, it could force us public, or get another partner involved, someone impossible to work with. There are plenty of ways he could ruin me. And normally he'd never do any of that to his own son, but he and Mom are so obsessed with the idea of carrying on the lineage..."

"You really think he'd do that, if you didn't give him what he wants?"

John winces and bows his head. It's answer enough. My stomach churns. But he just shakes his head again. "Like I said, my parents, all of this... it shouldn't be your concern. I'm sorry to drag you into all this."

I tighten my grip on his hand. "You're right," I say. "It was selfish to drag me into this..." I step closer, and his eyes find mine, pain written all over his face. It's enough to make my chest ache, and I long to do whatever it takes to wipe that pain from his expression. "You should have let me choose for myself," I say. "You should have told me everything so I could make my own decision. Because..." I lift his hand to my mouth and kiss the back of his knuckles softly. "I would have chosen to help you," I murmur softly.

Something flashes in his gaze then. *Hope.* "You'd have done that for me?"

"I still might." I arch an eyebrow. "If given the chance."

I'm not sure what I expect. Whatever it is, it's not this.

John goes down on one knee before me. My hand is still wrapped in his, and he holds up the ring I just shoved back at him. "Mara, my wife. Let me make this right, please. You know everything now. Give me a real chance to marry you, properly." A small smile touches his lips. "Since you don't really remember the first time, I don't think it counts."

My cheeks flush, and I can't help it. I laugh a little, my gaze fixed on his.

"Mrs. Mara Walloway," he says, and just the sound of that, of what my name could be if I say yes to this, sends a flutter of excitement through my body, into my belly. I swallow hard around a sudden lump in my throat, not sure

Overnight Wife 119

where it even came from. "Marry me," he whispers, and I can't resist the smile that spreads across my face.

"Well," I whisper, "if you insist."

He laughs, and I tighten my grip on his hand, and he rises, pulling me against him. Our lips crash together, and I swear he tastes even better than I remember, as he reaches up to cup the back of my head, pulling me closer to him, his lips parting mine and his tongue slipping between my lips, exploring my mouth, soft and slow and searing all at once.

I shut my eyes, and I sink into his kiss. Into my husband's arms.

11

JOHN

I check the clock. Only five minutes have passed. I could have sworn it had been about a million hours. But time always seems to crawl at moments like this—at times when all I want to do is be with Mara again. I've been working overtime tonight, the same way I had to three times already this week. Normally Mara would be doing the same, and I could sneak away down to the shop to distract her from her current project... But tonight she left early, promising to meet me later for dinner.

Which leaves me all alone in this empty office with no distractions. Not until I'm able to finish this pile of work and escape, at any rate.

With effort, I tear my gaze from the clock and turn back to my computer screen. The faster I work, the faster I get to leave, and the sooner I get to see her again. To get my hands on my beautiful, sexy as hell wife.

Just the thought is enough to make my dick stir. I remember the last time she came by my office after hours. She wore that same sexy blue dress she wore to meet my parents, only this time, I didn't let her wear it for long. I pinned her against the door almost before it had closed, and slid my hands up, pushing that dress up over her hips as my fingers toyed with the hem of her panties. I slid one finger beneath them, ran it along the edges of her pussy lips, and found her already soaking wet for me.

My dirty girl. She's always as eager as I am, every time we reunite. It's like neither of us can get enough, like we're dying of thirst in the desert, and we're each an oasis.

My cock hardens against the seam of my pants. I know I need to keep working, need to finish this and get out of here. But I can't help the way my mind drifts. Toward thoughts of Mara last night, and the sheer nightgown she wore. The way she posed across my bed when I got out of the shower wearing only a towel.

I dropped the towel the second I saw her, and I was already getting hard. Harder still when she spread her legs and ran her hand up the inside of her creamy thigh, her fingers inching higher and higher up that sexy, soft skin of hers. She parted her legs and let me see she was naked under that nightgown. She ran her fingers along her slit, toying with herself, parting her lips, her tongue tracing the edges of her teeth as I watched.

God, she looked so fucking sexy. It's a wonder I didn't pin her down right there, but I was patient. I was enjoying the show, after all.

She lay back on the bed and started to finger herself, gasping softly with each stroke. That was when I couldn't stand it anymore. I bent over her and took her hand, drawing it from her pussy and licking her finger clean slowly, my tongue hot against her skin, as I savored the salty sweet taste, her finger already coated in her juices.

I spread her legs then and pushed that nightgown up around her waist. Gripped the base of my cock tightly in one

Overnight Wife   123

fist and guided myself to her entrance. With my other hand, I caught her wrists and pinned her arms over her head, telling her exactly where I wanted her, waiting for her to spread her legs wider for me, hooking her ankles around my waist, before I plunged into her.

God, that sexy little scream of hers undid me.

It's enough to make me undo the top button of my jeans now, my hand stroking the edges of my cock through my boxers. *Mara. Mara, Mara, Mara...*

She's all I think about. All day. It's like I've been infected; like I'm addicted to that woman. And not only that, I'm lucky enough to call her my wife. I don't know how I got so damn lucky, but I'm not about to waste it.

I slide my hand into my boxers, shutting my eyes to picture her face last night. That sexy little part between her top and bottom lips as she gasped. That soft mouth of hers, and the way her body arched up against me, her breasts digging into my hard chest when I drove into her again and again...

I start to stroke my shaft, my fist tight around the hard steel of it. I stroke my thumb over the top, feeling a bead of precum already gathered there, that's how fucking horny this woman makes me.

I'm working myself up toward an edge when my door flings open without so much as a knock. My eyes jump to the doorframe, expecting to see Mara standing there, eager to call her over if it is, to have her join in.

But then I freeze.

It's not Mara. It's Bianca. *Fuck.*

There's a desk in my way, blocking my cock from view— at least, so I hope—but still, it's pretty obvious what I was just doing. I shove my pants closed again, and the zipper sounds deafeningly loud in this tight space, far too obvious.

Still, I clear my throat and hope the flush doesn't show on my cheeks.

"Bianca. Can I help you with something?"

"I'm so sorry," she blurts. "I didn't realize you were... um, that it would be a bad time." Her face is bright red. Probably even redder than mine.

Still, she steps into the office, and shuts the door behind her slowly.

"What is it you need?" I ask, crossing one leg over the other to hide the inconvenient, still obvious bulge.

Her gaze drops toward the desk anyway, and to what I'm concealing behind it. "Nothing important. It was just a silly question about budgets, it can wait... until a better time..." She hesitates and glances up at me again, before she bites her lower lip slowly. "Unless, of course, this is a good time."

I frown. "A good time for what?"

She hesitates again. Takes a deep breath. And then she steps toward my desk. Closer to me. "A good time for us to talk. About..." Her gaze darts down again. "Other things."

"Bianca..."

But she's already at my desk. Sliding onto it, in a way that all too obviously hikes up the hem of her skirt, revealing a clear slash of thigh. She's not my type, never has been. But the move makes me wonder exactly how many higher-ups she's used it on before now. "I wouldn't blame you, if you were getting bored in here all by yourself. Or lonely." She glances down again, pointedly, before her gaze locks back onto mine, her lips curved in a sly smile. "I can help distract you, boss."

"No," I say, more harshly than I meant for it to come out. I clear my throat with difficulty and rise from my chair. At least this conversation has been helping to kill my boner at a possibly record-breaking speed. "Bianca,

Overnight Wife   125

whatever you think is happening here... it isn't. Please leave."

Her face flushes bright red, before it goes blanched and pale, emotions chasing themselves across her face. Surprise, then embarrassment... But she settles on anger by the end. Shoves off my desk with her fists balled. "Oh, so you prefer the butch muscular type, is that it?"

Not exactly words I'd use to describe Mara, but I can catch her drift. "I prefer my wife," I respond coolly.

"She's not good enough for you. Isn't that obvious?" Bianca raises her chin, eyes narrowed.

It's enough to spark fury in my own veins in response. "You need to leave. Now."

She flashes me a furious glare as she storms toward the door. "You think you've had it tough, John Walloway?" Her voice comes out tight and angry. "You should learn what it really feels like to have your life ruined. Then we'd see how tough you really are. Or aren't, without the whole world catering to your every whim..."

I don't answer that. But when she slams the door behind her with one last glare, something sparks inside me.

Fear.

All I can think about is Mara. Mara, safe but oblivious at home, getting ready for our dinner date. *You should learn what it really feels like to have your life ruined...* What did she mean by that? What did she do?

I'm grabbing my desk phone before I even have time to think about it. I dial Mara's number off by heart, one of the only phone numbers I bothered to memorize. It rings once, twice, and my breath hitches in my chest. *No, don't let anything have happened to her.* I couldn't face that possibility, couldn't handle it if something had happened...

But then I hear her familiar voice on the other end of the

line. "Hello?"

"Mara, it's me. Are you on your way to dinner yet?"

I can hear honking in the background, the sound of traffic. "I'm in the car. Why, what's the matter?"

"Nothing. I'm fine."

"You don't sound fine," she points out, in the way that I normally love of hers, of seeing straight through my crap. In spite of my worry, I have to smile.

"No, it's..." I shake my head. I'm being paranoid. Overprotective. I'm worrying about nothing, that's all. "Something strange just happened, that's all," I say. "I'll explain when we're at dinner, all right?"

"Okay," she says, still with that hesitation in her tone. "You sure you're fine?"

"I'll see you soon," I say, mostly to avoid having to lie to her over that question again. "When you get to the restaurant, stay put, okay? I don't want you off somewhere by yourself just now, that's all."

A long pause on the other end of the line, followed by a sigh. "Okay, but you're explaining what the hell is going on the second you get here."

"I know," I tell her. "I promise." I hang up and shut down my computer, reaching for my coat. There's still more work I'd planned on finishing before I left tonight, but screw it. First priorities have to come first. And there's a nagging sense of worry I can't shake, a fear that there's something wrong here that I'm not seeing right now. It's a worry I know I won't be able to shake until I'm with Mara, until I have her in my arms and I know she's all right.

So, leaving work unfinished, something I've never done since the day I started Pitfire years ago, I shut off my office lights, lock the door carefully behind me, and head downstairs toward my car, to go and find my wife.

12

JOHN

She's standing outside the restaurant when I pull up. It's a nicer place, a new one that just opened in town, which we'd both been eager to try. But right now, the restaurant and its well-reviewed fare is the last thing on my mind. I toss my keys to the valet without even looking, and beeline straight toward Mara, not stopping until I wrap my arms around her slender form and pull her against me.

She laughs softly, her face buried in my chest, the vibration of her laughter traveling up through my arms and chest, sending my head buzzing with the fresh proximity of her. I dip down to kiss the top of her head and try my best not to get distracted by how amazing she smells—rose shampoo mixed with her jasmine perfume and the scent beneath them both, a sweet smell that's all my wife.

"There you are," I murmur against her hair, and she laughs again, drawing back just far enough to tilt her chin up and catch my gaze, her eyes narrowed with confusion and more than a little bit of suspicion.

"What's going on?" she asks. "Are you all right?"

"I am now that I know you are," I tell her, my arms tightening around her once more.

She tilts her head back, and I bend down to kiss her forehead, then the tip of her nose, and finally her lips, soft and slow. She lets out a sigh and sinks into me a little more closely, just for a second. Then she twists out of my grasp. "Are you going to explain the freak out, or are you going to leave me in suspense all night?"

I grimace and slide my hands down her arms before I take her hand, leading her toward the front of the restaurant. "Bianca came onto me."

"*What*?" Mara's eyebrows shoot upward.

I explain everything. The office. What I'd been daydreaming about—in a low voice, but enough detail to make her blush and check our surroundings to make sure nobody could overhear. We reach the maître d' stand then, and I pause long enough to give him our name and watch the man's expression shift from surprise to eagerness. He leads us through the restaurant, to a little back room I reserved for a private chef's tasting.

After more than enough pampering to drive us both crazy, asking every ten seconds if either of us need anything else from him, the man finally leaves us in peace. It's only once we're alone again that I resume the story.

I tell her about Bianca walking in on me, and her flirtation. Then I add how I rejected her, and what she said afterward.

All the while, Mara toys with her menu with one hand, frowning, her eyes on the table and her thoughts apparently a million miles away. Finally, unable to stand the tension, or the guilt that's sitting like a rock in my stomach right now, I shift in my chair, leaning closer to Mara.

Overnight Wife

"Did I lead her on? I swear, I haven't flirted with her, or said anything to make her think we've been anything but colleagues this whole time... But maybe I was giving off signals unconsciously, maybe I said something in the wrong tone—"

"You're being too hard on yourself," Mara cuts in. "I've seen the two of you together. You never did anything wrong, John, trust me. I'd have called you on it way before now if you had." A touch of a smile ghosts across her face.

I grimace in response. "But that reaction of hers... Saying I should learn what it's like to have my life ruined?" I scowl.

"An overreaction, definitely." Mara sighs. "She was probably hurt, embarrassed, angry you didn't fancy her the way she fancied you..." Mara shakes her head. "Crushes make people do stupid things."

"Believe me, that much I know." I manage a smirk.

Mara rolls her eyes and kicks me under the table. Then her expression shifts into a sly smile. "I'm flattered you thought of me so quickly, though."

"Even if it was to over react and freak out that you were in some kind of danger?" I point out, eyes narrowing.

She laughs. "Of course. It's kind of sexy how protective you are."

"You have no idea, wife." I reach down under the table, my hand tracing along her thigh. She's wearing jeans again, like she normally does, but that's never stopped me before. My hand inches higher, and her lips part a little as her eyes dart around the restaurant. Or at least, the small back room where we're seated.

"John..."

"I asked for this room for a reason," I reply, my smile

widening. "Privacy is key, when you're a big-name celebrity like me."

She smirks, rolling her eyes. "Oh God, the ego has finally gone to your head."

"What can I say? I'm used to getting what I want, when I want it." I lean toward her, my lips catching her temple, then sliding down her cheek. "And what I want right now, Mara, is my sexy wife."

She shivers and tilts toward me, her body shifting against mine. "You sure about that? You don't want to flirt with anybody else?" She says it lightly, like a joke, but it makes that rock of guilt shift in me again, and I pull back, just far enough so that I can see her face, my eyes locked on hers.

"Mara, I would never flirt with anyone else."

She laughs. "Relax, John. I know that."

"Still." I frown. "I feel like I wronged you somehow. Just, that whole interaction..."

She shakes her head. "Don't think about it." She leans in to kiss me, then, her lips soft and sweet against mine. "You didn't do anything wrong." She reaches up to cup my cheek, her hands soft against my stubble. "You're a good man, John Walloway. And an even better husband."

I smile and turn to kiss the open palm of her hand. My gaze drifts down for a second, to the ring she's wearing again, now that the shallow cut on her ring finger has finally healed. We got it resized a little, so that it fits properly, not too tightly or in a way that might injure her again.

I have to admit, it looks beautiful on her. But even better is the knowledge of what it means. Of how it marks her as mine. *My* wife. I don't plan on ever letting her go.

"I love you, Mara," I whisper, feeling every word of that.

Her eyes go wide, fixed as they are on mine. I can see her pupils dilate, watch the way her breath catches in her chest as she takes in the full meaning of that.

"I love you," I repeat, reaching up to cup her face between my palms. I lean in to kiss her again, to taste her mouth, those perfect shell lips of hers soft and pillowy on mine.

When we part, her lips remain parted a breath, her throat working with a tight swallow. Then her gaze leaps to mine once more. "I love you too, John," she breathes.

God, she's so beautiful.

And I'm so fucking hard right now. I don't hesitate. I slide my hands down her curves and draw her toward me. I pull her onto my lap, until she's straddling me, one knee on either side of my chair, the menus discarded and forgotten on the table beside us.

I reach down between us to undo the top button of her jeans, my fingers grazing the smooth plane of her belly underneath her shirt. She tenses at my touch, arching her hips toward me, her back curving in a way that makes me unable to resist sliding my hands up along the small of her back, tracing that arch, dragging her down against me.

With my other hand, I cup the back of her neck and draw her into another kiss, slow and searing. At the same time, I undo the zip of her jeans the rest of the way, reach my hand between us and into her pants, sliding my fingers down to cup her pussy tightly, hard and sudden.

She gasps and arches against me, grinding into my palm with abandon. Her hair cascades down her back, free and wild, just like her.

"God you're so fucking sexy," I whisper, and she smiles at me, her eyes dark with desire. I shift my hand against her, starting to rub her pussy through her panties, already able to feel how wet they are with her lust.

"You… drive me wild," she murmurs, in that sexy, throaty voice that I love, when she's turned on and can't resist anymore.

I push the thin, soaking wet fabric of her panties aside and trace my finger along the lips of her pussy, one at a time, teasing, going lightly. "I can tell," I say, one eyebrow arched. "You're always so wet for me, dirty girl."

She licks her lips, and the movement, the track of her tongue, draws my eye, makes me think about all the things she does with that tongue. At the same time, her hands slide down between us, and she traces the bulge of my cock through my jeans. "And you're already hard just thinking about me, aren't you, husband?" The word husband sends an extra pulse of white-hot desire through me.

This is what I wanted earlier tonight, alone in my office. I wanted her hands on me, touching me, tightening around me. More than that, I wanted to be inside her.

I shift my hands out of her jeans, ignoring her faint little mewl of protest, and wrap my hands around her thighs instead. Her eyes flash to mine with surprise, just before I rise from the seat and push her back against the table, sending the menus onto the floor.

Her eyes dart to the door, but I smile, shaking my head. "Nobody will come in until we call them," I say. "I made sure of that."

I knew I'd want Mara all to myself tonight. The same way I do every night, any time we're alone together.

She smiles, shaking her head a little. "You're so naughty."

"You like it," I point out, grinning, as I work her jeans down off of her hips.

Overnight Wife   133

"Hmm, maybe," she says, but the words are undermined by the fact that her breath comes out as a faint sigh, her body already pliable with want. I push her jeans the rest of the way off, until they puddle under the table at our feet, and her bare ass is on the table, only her thin little thong between her and me now.

Her hands drift to the front of my jeans and start on my buttons next.

"Do you know what torture it is?" I ask her. "To work with you every day and not be able to touch you the whole long time."

She smirks. "I don't know... You seem to find a way to sneak in touches now and again."

"Not nearly enough," I tell her. "I can never get enough of you." She lets out a gasp then, because I've pulled her to the edge of the table, my thumbs hooking under her panties. I yank them down and off, in a quick move that makes her breath come faster, her pulse beating so quickly I can feel it in her throat when I bend down to kiss my way over her skin, nipping her gently every so often, lashing her with my tongue in between, until her toes curl and her body arches against my hands.

I trail my hands up to her chest, run my thumbs along the hard little bulges of her nipples, which I can feel through her shirt and her thin athletic bra. She twists against me, and finally manages to coordinate her hands enough to push my jeans off. I step out of them with a grin, and she pushes my boxers down after, her hands going right where I want them a second later.

She wraps her hands tightly around the base of my cock, and God, just that simple touch of hers is enough to light me on fire.

"I want to fuck you," I whisper, my eyes on hers. "Right here, right now."

Her gaze drifts again, and I know what she's thinking. About the rest of the restaurant out there, behind just a simple separator door, close enough to risk them hearing everything. "What if people hear?" she replies, worrying at her lower lip.

"I don't care," I say, and my free hand goes around her waist, pinning her in place. With the other, I spread her thighs and drag my thumb lightly along her clit. "I want them to know you're mine."

She gasps and tilts toward me, her lips parted, her face flushed with heat and desire.

I could stare at her like this all day long. Flushed and naked and waiting for me. But she's right. We are in public. Which means I'll have to be a little quicker. And if I make her moan a little too loudly in doing so, well... so it goes.

I guide myself toward her entrance, and her hands stay tight around my cock, shifting with me, stroking me a little. Making me harder than ever.

"I love you," I whisper again, this time as the tip of my cock reaches her entrance, and I shift my hips toward the table, easing into her.

Her eyelids flutter, and she drops my cock to reach up and wrap her arms around my shoulders instead, bracing herself. "John..." Her eyes go wide, then, as I grip her hips with both hands and drive myself harder into her, deeper. Her pussy stretches tight around me, so deliciously wet and warm and hungry. I pull back a little, thrust deeper. Again and again until I'm buried all the way inside her, my cock filling her pussy, stretching her walls, making her feel stuffed full. "I love you," she breathes too, then, her eyes still fixed on mine, wide and hot.

Overnight Wife   135

The words flood me with heat. She's mine—really mine. Not just an accidental marriage or some ploy to appease my family. *She's my wife.* I grin and bend her over beneath me, driving into her faster now, turned on by the thought, by the feel of her beneath me, opening up to me, her head falling back and her mouth parting as she gasps for breath.

I reach down between us, and my fingertips barely brush her clit before she's crying out, unable to help herself as the orgasm sweeps through her. My grin widens, and I reach up to press a hand over her mouth, muffling the sound, as I continue to fuck her, harder, angling myself to be sure my cock drags along her inner walls, adding to her pleasure.

"That's it, my sexy wife," I whisper, my voice almost a growl with all the desire and heat I'm suppressing right now. "Come for me."

She doesn't need telling twice. Not as I fuck her so hard my balls slap against her pussy and her ass bounces against the table. Before long she's at the edge again, then coming once more, with an even louder cry this time, one I have to press hard against her lips to muffle.

"Fuck, Mara, you're incredible." My eyes lock on her, drinking her in.

It doesn't take me long to finish after that—just the sight of her, flushed, her chest heaving for breath, her legs locked around me, her pussy wet and as tight as a fist around my cock, is enough to get me close. I finish with a deep guttural growl, burying my cock in her and pulling her body against mine, holding her there as I come inside her, coating her, our juices mingling and dripping down her thighs when we draw apart.

She arches an eyebrow, eyeing the table, and we both laugh. "Oh God. We have to clean this up before we eat here." Her cheeks flare bright red, and she glances at the door to the rest of the restaurant. As if that flimsy piece of wood will have kept anyone outside from figuring out exactly what we were doing back here.

It makes me smile, even though I know she's embarrassed by it after the fact. Because I *want* people to hear. I want them to know how sexy my wife is. How impossible it is to keep my hands off her.

Hell, I want the whole damn world to know Mara is mine. Deep down, I'm not upset about that article coming out, or about whichever of my crappy relatives spilled the beans to the press about our relationship.

Because it brings this whole thing one step closer to real. It brings *her* one step closer to officially being mine, for good. Forever.

"It's fine," I tell her, helping her down off the table and picking up her bra to pass her. "See?" I drop my napkin over the mess and laugh at her horrified expression. Then I catch her around the waist and tug her against me, leaning in to whisper against the nape of her neck. "Why don't we just get takeout after all?"

Her eyes dart around us, as she's no doubt considering the class of restaurant, we're in. One of the best in the city. One with a wait list miles long. "Do they let people do that?"

"They'll let *us,*" I say. Her brow furrows a little, but I lean in to kiss it away, already taking out a hundred-dollar bill to leave on the table as tip. "Don't worry," I murmur against her forehead. "I'm sure they'll understand why I couldn't keep my hands off my sexy wife for a minute longer."

"I'm pretty sure they'll guess you failed at that," she points out, but she's laughing now, even as she pulls on her clothes. She lets out a sigh, her bangs fluttering against her forehead, and shoots me a sideways look. "I'm going to have to get used to attracting a lot of attention, aren't I?"

Overnight Wife

I try and fail not to grin. "Probably." I arch an eyebrow. "Is that a deal-breaker, wife?"

"Not at all, husband. I just want to be sure what I'm really getting into here. If..." She hesitates. Eyes me once more, almost like she's afraid I'm going to bolt if she looks at this whole situation too closely. "If we're really doing this thing."

I know the feeling. I've had similar feelings. Especially the other day when she threw her ring back at me. But the fear I felt at the idea of losing her? It only makes me more certain that this—that *she*—is what I want.

I step closer to her and sweep her into my arms, crushing her against my chest as she wraps her arms around my neck, holding on tight. "I want this, Mara," I whisper against her hair. "I want *you*. What I feel for you is real."

She tilts her head back, a sly smile on her lips. "Who would have guessed?" she murmurs. "An accidental marriage between two strangers could turn into true love."

"And yet here we are." I smile and lean in to kiss her again, softer and slower this time, taking my time to enjoy her. I'm already starting to swell again, just at the sensation of her hands wrapped around my neck, her body pressed to mine. But it's more than just attraction or lust. It's *happiness*.

I've never felt this way before. Not even with Heather, back when I thought I knew what love was. This blows every other woman I've dated, every other love I've experienced, out of the water. The woman who caught my eye in that club in Las Vegas; the wild party girl who was willing to run away to the chapel with me, drunk and exhilarated and just looking to celebrate her new lease on life, the new job she was about to plunge into... She turned out to be the perfect woman for me.

The woman I never knew I'd been waiting for, all along.

When she nestles into my arms, her head resting on my chest, letting out a sigh of sheer pleasure, that's when I know. I will do anything to make her exactly as happy as she is right now, for the rest of our lives.

This is it for me. She's it.

13

MARA

A calendar alert reminds me of something I'd almost forgotten in the whirlwind of the last week with John. Our deadline to annul is coming up. Two days. That's all I have left to change my mind about this. To step off the crazy train and declare our marriage null and void—before reality sets in, and this all becomes real. Our wedding, our marriage, everything.

But in a move that might be even more crazy than our marriage was in the first place... I don't want to.

I want to stay with John. I want to give this a real shot.

So I close the reminder with a sigh and a smile, about to turn back to my work. I'm in the office early again, as usual, hard at work in the wood shop, awaiting the rest of my coworkers to arrive. I've started coming in earlier than I used to, mostly to avoid the stares when I first arrive, the judgment on everyone else's face.

Daniel has finally started acting semi-normal around me again, saying—when I finally dared to ask what he thought about me and John—that he'd just been surprised by the secret, that was all. But pretty much everyone else acts cold as ice around me. And don't even get me started on Bianca. I haven't seen her face to face since the night John tracked me down the restaurant in a panic and told me she came on to him. I think—hope—that she's embarrassed by her behavior. But who knows?

Ever since that night, she's avoided the wood shop, stayed glued to her desk on the far side of the office, and dodges my glances, even going so far as to pretend to be on the phone anytime I'm within her vicinity.

I tell myself I don't care. That I'll get used to it. That my other colleagues will come around when we work together longer and they realize I'm dedicated to this job; that I didn't just sleep my way into it. But for now... it rankles, I won't lie.

It's the only wrinkle in the otherwise shockingly perfect fabric of this life John and I have unexpectedly started together. When it's just us together, or out with friends... the rest of the bullshit fades away. It's just us, and I know this is right. It *feels* right, in a way I've never experienced before. In a way that makes me never want to let go.

I shake myself with a start, realizing that I'm just staring at my phone calendar daydreaming. But it's when I shake myself out of it that my gaze lands on the date again. Double check it. Triple check.

My stomach does a backflip. *Fuck*. Is that the date?

My heart starts to hammer faster, my earlier thoughts forgotten as I tap on another app I installed a while back, a tracker, one I added just out of curiosity. Now, though, it's coming in handy.

I check the dates again, do the math, and swear once more under my breath, softly.

I'm late. My period is late.

I swallow hard, wracking my brain. I take birth control, but

Overnight Wife

141

I'm not exactly the best at sticking to strict schedules, especially since I've been working so much. Sometimes I take it in the mornings, sometimes in the evenings... John and I stopped using condoms since the two of us are definitely exclusive. But it never even occurred to me to worry about anything happening.

I'd been so focused on work, on figuring out what we wanted to happen with our marriage, that I didn't even think about anything more practical.

My stomach churns, unsettled. It's almost 9am, almost time for my coworkers to arrive. The last thing I want to face right now is anybody else walking in on me in the midst of figuring out this revelation. I grab my cell phone and beeline out of the office, waiting until I'm safely away from the entrance in the parking lot to dial.

Lea picks up on the second ring, sounding groggy. "Who is this early bird and what has she done with my best friend?" she grumbles into the line.

"I'm late," I say, without any other greeting. "My period, it's late."

There's a long beat of silence, followed by shuffling, the crumple of sheets. Lea crawling out of bed, most likely. Her bartending gig means that she works late nights and usually doesn't rise before the crack of noon. I feel a little guilty for waking her this early, but any guilt is overshadowed by my growing worry.

"Well, at least you're married, so it won't be a bastard," she says, after a long moment, and I half-laugh, half-groan into the phone. "Kidding, Mara. Deep breaths, okay? Don't freak out until you know for sure if you are. Go to the store, get a test."

"And then?"

"And then, figure out what you want to do." There's

another sound. A shower turning on in the background. "I mean, you told me John was pretty baby crazy, right?"

"No, I told you his *family* is," I clarify. "And crazy would be an understatement when it comes to his mother." I can still picture that heap of gifts. Her face as she told me I owed them a baby, in exchange for being *kept*. Like I was some kind of pet her son had adopted at the shelter and dragged home.

My stomach churns again. Would I want to bring a child into that world?

But then I think about John. I think about his face when he talked about finding a wife, settling down. Or the way he looks at me, like I'm the only woman in the world who's ever ignited him. We work so well together—both in marriage and in our actual work. If there's anyone in the whole world I could picture myself having a family with, it's him. He's someone who would actually participate fully, who wouldn't leave me to care for the kid all on my own, but who would take an equal role in parenting. I'm sure of it.

But... the weight settles like lead in my stomach. I think about my career. Everything I've worked for. My whole life, which is really only just beginning. Can I really derail that? With a change as huge as this?

Then again. Look at my marriage, and how badly I thought it would derail me. When in fact, meeting and accidentally marrying John might have been the best decision of my life. If anything, it only improved my life—my whole life, not just the career I'd always been focused on to the point of ignoring the rest of my needs.

"I can hear those wheels of yours churning. What are you thinking?" On the other end, I hear splashes, no doubt as Lea ducks into her shower.

I sigh into the receiver. "I don't know, Lea. I don't know

Overnight Wife

what I want to do. I never thought I'd want a family this young—someday, sure, but now? But then, I think about John, about having a family with *him* specifically, and... I don't know."

There's another long pause, followed by the telltale slosh of bathwater, before Lea's voice returns closer to the microphone. "Well, take the test. Like I said, no use making plans until you know. And once you do know, you can make an informed decision, with all the facts. Yeah?"

"You're right." I tilt my head back to squint up at the blue sky overhead. It's shaping up to be a beautiful day. Too pretty to be stressing like this, at least until, like she says, I know the truth. "What if I am though?" I murmur. "How the hell am I going to tell him?"

"A card is always nice," she replies, and I burst into laughter.

"Thanks for the pep talk."

"Call me with the results?" she asks before I disconnect.

"Of course. Soon as I know." I hang up and tug my car keys from my pocket, jangling them between my fingers. Time to face the music.

* * *

Well. I should have guessed it.

I squat in the bathroom of the CVS, staring at the test in my fingers. Staring, more specifically, at the thin pink line that marks a sharp and sudden divide in my life. Before and after. As in, before I went and got myself knocked up by my new husband, and after I realized that this already complicated as hell mess is about to get a million times more complicated.

I shoot Lea a text, aware that I promised to call her. But I can't handle hearing her voice right now. Even my best friend's reassurances won't help. Not now.

I shut my eyes and ignore the phone as it buzzes away in my lap. Lea tries twice more before she gives up and texts me back instead.

Never doubt the power of a well-worded card, is all she says, clearly deciding to opt on the side of lighthearted. She knows me too well. She knows that I can't handle looking at this seriously right now.

But the words draw a laugh out of me anyway, albeit a reluctant one.

Still. It's not the worst idea. I'm going to have to tell John somehow. And in spite of us deciding that we want to really seriously try to make this marriage work... I'm still not entirely sure how he's going to handle news like this. News this huge.

I deposit the test in the trash and trudge out to my car, hands tucked into my pockets. Along the way, I stop in the CVS card section and buy a card. I labor and debate over the type—Congratulations? Condolences? Thank you for the baby? Sorry, but guess what?

Finally, I settle on one of the blank cards, the front covered in glitter and flowers. At least it doesn't have any cheesy pre-written messages inside. I want to write my own, although what exactly I plan to say, I'm still not sure. How do you explain something like this?

I spend the whole drive back to work thinking it over, my brow furrowed. When I get to the office, it's late—the only parking spot available is pretty far from the front. But that's fine. It gives me more time to think. I pull into it and shut off the car, then lean my head on the steering wheel, eyes shut, hands gripping the leather, and force my tired brain to *think*.

Under all my fear and worries, there's an undercurrent

Overnight Wife   145

of emotion I can't ignore. An undercurrent of... *happiness.* Because that's how I feel when I'm with John. And if that's how I feel with him, just the two of us, then how much happier will I feel when it's three of us? When we have a family. When our marriage becomes indisputably, permanently, real.

Finally, the right words come to me. I pull the card out and prop it on the dashboard, starting to write.

I lay it all out. How I feel about him, which came out of nowhere, as unexpected as the wild night that led to our marriage. And I end with how I'm feeling now—like this could be the same situation. Something wild and unexpected... but right. Something that could improve both our lives, as long as we keep our priorities straight. As long as we're both all in.

When I finish, signing it feels wrong. So I draw something instead. It's been a while since I've set ink to paper—I used to sketch out all my set designs in detail before I worked on them, but nowadays I work from computer renderings instead. Still, it comes back to me easily enough, with the pen in my hand.

I draw John, the way I remember him best. Lying beside me in bed, his dark eyes steady and fixed on mine. Reassuring me that whatever happens, he'll be here for me.

Just like I'll be here for him, no matter what happens now. No matter where this news takes the two of us in life.

When I'm finished, I leave the card sitting open on my dashboard and root around for the card's envelope. When I find it, I tuck it inside and write on the front in swirling script, John's name. Then I grab my purse and move to climb out of my car, only to let out a gasp of surprise.

Bianca is standing outside my car, her eyes huge and round with shock, fixed on me.

No. Fixed on the card in my hand.

She moves back as I shove open my door and climb out of the car. I expect her to run away, the way she's been doing around me ever since the night she hit on John. But she stands her ground, to my surprise, and fixes her attention on the envelope in my hand instead. "I'm sorry, I didn't mean to pry, but I was walking past, and I saw you... you seemed a little ill, so I came to check..." But she doesn't meet my gaze. She just stares at the envelope in my hand, with John's name on the front. "Did I read that right?" she asks. "Are you pregnant?"

The fear and worry I've been battling all day turn to jagged rocks in my stomach. I press the card over my heart, like that can shield me. "What do you want?" I snap.

Her cheeks flush. "I wanted to apologize," she says, and it's so far from what I expected that my eyebrows shoot upward.

"What?"

She clears her throat, and finally, finally, drags her eyes up to meet mine. "I'm sorry. About what happened with John and me. I'm sure he told you; I was just so embarrassed about it all... I thought he was flirting with me; clearly, I was wrong. I shouldn't have made a move." Her eyes drift to the envelope again. "Do you need anything? Can I help somehow?"

But I shake my head, moving away from her. She may have apologized for hitting on John—for misreading his signals, supposedly—but that doesn't change the fact that she hit on him *after* she found out he and I were married. Even if our marriage was a sham, where is the respect in that?

And then there's the last week at work. A whole week where she ignored me, refused to even acknowledge

Overnight Wife   147

anything had happened. And now she wants to apologize and act like everything is fine... why? Because she found out I'm pregnant? Because she pities me? "I'm fine," I say coldly, turning toward the building.

"Good luck," she calls behind me, but I know her well enough to hear the catch in her tone. The insincerity.

Screw her. Screw her advice, her telling me that everyone at Pitfire thinks I married John for this job. They don't know anything, and neither does she.

Back in the building, I tuck the card into my purse, planning to give it to John later tonight. Once everyone else clears out of the building. For now, I have work to do, and thanks to my much longer than usual morning break at the pharmacy, I'll be playing catch-up.

I bypass the workshop for once and head straight into the theater. We've been hard at work creating all the pieces for this play, but this week, we'll be starting to actually assemble the stage itself. It's an exciting step, usually my favorite part of set design. It's when all the pieces you've labored on so much, all the disparate puzzle pieces stacked up inside your head, finally join together on stage into something that starts to resemble a real theater. It's when your imagination finally gets to come to life.

But today, I'm distracted. I force a smile and a wave for Daniel, and chat to a few of our stage hands about the order of setup. I want to get the background design right first, before we start adding the smaller set pieces to it. There's one in particular, a moving set piece, that I'm worried about making fit. It needs to be suspended over the stage on wires, but accessible, because at one part of the play, toward the end of the second act, it needs to be able to move—to swing into the set, and be sturdy enough for one of the actors to climb onto it. It's supposed to look like a series of stars in the night sky, at least until it swings down and reveals itself to be a chariot made out of shooting stars.

It'll be the trickiest part of our design, but I have faith we can pull it off.

I leave a couple stage hands, overseen by Daniel, in charge of getting that whole thing hooked into the strap and pulley system we designed to hoist it up. We'll test it a couple of times, before we hoist it all the way into position.

In the meantime, I get started helping some other employees prop up the background itself. When I get in, they're already halfway done hanging the various deer antler designs John and I sculpted by hand onto what will become the back wall of the cabin where most of the first act takes place.

My heart skips a little, touching those pieces again. Remembering the way John's hands cupped the clay around mine, the way he shaped them alongside me... And the way he pushed them aside to run his hands over me afterward, until it felt like he was sculpting me too, tracing my body until it became real, as molded as the clay we'd been working with.

I'm lost in memories of that, of his hands over mine, guiding mine, or letting me guide him, both in equal measure, when I hear raised voices. I finish attaching the set of antlers I'd been working on to its place on the back wall of the "cabin," and then turn to spot Bianca passing out the usual round of afternoon coffees to the crew. I hadn't seen her do this in a while. It makes me pause, uncertain.

Maybe I was being too harsh on her earlier, ignoring her olive branch of an apology. But I just don't trust her. Not after everything she did.

I'm about to turn away, back to my work, when I hear a shout, from the opposite side of the stage this time. I whip

Overnight Wife 149

around and spot Daniel barking angry orders at one of the guys he was supervising. The guy is swearing, grabbing at a rope... My eyes trace the rope up, widening with every foot they travel into the rafters.

Oh, shit.

They hoisted the chariot already. Even though I told them to be sure to only test it a few feet off the ground first. To judge by Daniel's cursing, he didn't order this either. But there's no time to worry about whose fault it is, because when my eyes trace the trajectory of the chariot, I realize what's about to happen.

The ropes it's tied to are fraying. The wooden construction is heavier than we wagered. And standing right beneath it, in the path of the thing that's about to collapse onto her oblivious head, is Bianca, a stack of coffee in hand.

I don't pause to think about it. I react on sheer instinct. I sprint across the stage. Somewhere behind me, I hear more shouts, even a scream. That's enough to finally catch Bianca's attention and make her whip around to look at me, eyes widening. Then she looks up, and now she has the sense to scream too, just before I collide with her.

The force of my body crashing into her sends the coffees flying out of her hands and splashing across the stage. It also sends both of us toppling to the ground, just as, with a deafening snap, the chariot's rope finally gives way.

We hit the ground, Bianca beneath me. My head flies past hers though, cracks against the wood of the stage. I have just enough consciousness left to hear a deafening splinter as the chariot lands on the stage too, inches from us. Then the world spins and swirls into star bursts, before it fades to black.

14

JOHN

I'm on my way back from lunch break when my phone starts to ring. It's the office, though a line I don't recognize. Not any of my usual secretaries. I pick up, only to hear a harried, familiar male voice on the other end. Daniel.

"Get in here, right now," he says. "It's your wife."

If I'd been holding anything, I would have dropped it. As it is, I barely manage to hang onto my phone. I'd just parked my car, and I fly out of it now, not bothering to lock it behind me as I sprint toward Pitfire. Belatedly, I register the vehicle parked out front, lights flashing.

An ambulance.

Fuck.

Not Mara. Please, let her be safe.

I take the steps two at a time, and once I'm inside the building, I break into a flat out run toward the main stage. It's where Mara was supposed to be all day today, starting to put together the set she's been painstakingly preparing in pieces up until now. I know how excited she was about today. How much she enjoys putting a set together like this.

What's happened to ruin it?

I reach the theater and yank open the double doors at the back, only to nearly collide with a stretcher rolling out of the main entrance. My stomach sinks straight through my shoes and down into the floor. Lying across that stretcher, her eyes shut, an IV stuck into her arm... "Mara!" My voice breaks on that one word.

A paramedic grabs my arm, pulls me back. "Sir, we need to get through."

"That's my wife," I bark.

His grip on my arm relaxes a little, and his expression shifts to one of understanding. "She's all right, Mr. Walloway. It looks like just a concussion, but we're going to need to run some tests."

My gaze darts from her unconscious form to the stretcher, and then follows the thought out to the stage behind her. "What happened?" I bark, and my question isn't so much directed at the paramedic anymore as it is at the cluster of my employees scattered around the stage. I spot Bianca, pacing back and forth, her head in her hands, her whole body shaking. Near her, but not quite touching her, Daniel is holding something—a frayed piece of rope. There's wood in splinters all across the stage.

My stomach sinks. The wreckage looks bad. Was Mara in the middle of that?

The paramedic is handing me something. A card, with an address. "Follow us with her things," he says, and only when he says that do I register other things scattered across the stage. Mara's purse, a recognizable lump near the side of the stage, almost as if she dropped it in a panic and bolted. "Your wife is going to be fine, I promise."

It's an empty promise, I know. Nobody can promise that for anyone else. But still, it does relax me, just a little, to glance past this competent man toward my wife prone on

Overnight Wife   153

her stretcher, with those words in my ears. *She's going to be fine,* I repeat to myself, before I finally relax my hold on the paramedic and let him go to do his job. Let him take care of my Mara.

In the meantime, feeling less than useless, I pace toward the stage, glaring at everyone in my path.

"Explain what happened," I bark when I reach the stage itself. I grimace, looking at the wreckage. It looks like some wooden contraption fell from a height. It probably even damaged the floorboards of the stage itself. *Fuck.* This is going to be expensive. But as long as Mara is all right, that's all I care about.

"I don't know how it happened," Daniel is saying, as I cross behind him to scoop up Mara's things. Her purse. Her wallet. Some other items, including an envelope, that fell out of the purse itself.

I pause mid-gathering to glance at him. He holds up a frayed rope to demonstrate.

"It looks like somebody tampered with this. Cut part of the line to weaken it. But... who would do that?" Daniel's frown deepens.

But my gaze drifts past him, to where Bianca is sitting on the edge of the stage, rocking back and forth, her head in her hands, moaning a little. Suspicion crystalizes in my gut. I cross toward her, still holding Mara's things. When I get close enough, I can hear what Bianca's muttering under her breath.

"I didn't mean to hurt her; I didn't. I just wanted to scare her... Just a scare, that's all..."

With a scowl, I plant myself next to her, arms crossed. "Why," I say, loud enough to make Bianca jump and spin around, her eyes wide and fixed on me. "Why did you do this," I repeat, gesturing over my shoulder toward Daniel and the frayed rope he's holding.

Bianca stares at me, then him, and for a moment, I think she's going to deny it. Play dumb. It would probably come naturally to her. But then her throat works with a hard swallow, and she bows her head. "I didn't want to hurt anyone," she whispers into her lap.

"What did I ever do to you? What did *Mara* ever do?"

"Nothing," Bianca blurts. Then her eyes harden, and she sets her jaw. "It wasn't me you hurt. It was my sister."

I frown, confused. "What are you—"

"Heather."

I stare at her. *Of course.* Heather had an older half-sister, one she talked about often enough. Though she never mentioned her name. Their last names are different, too... But now that I'm looking, I see the resemblance. The hard set of Bianca's jaw, the flash in her eyes. "You're fired," I spit, too furious to say anything else. "You have fifteen minutes to get off my property before I call the police. And that is being generous, I hope you know," I add, when Bianca's eyes narrow in response.

At least she listens, though. She shoves off the stage, shoulders tense, and marches toward the exit.

"The rest of you, clean this up," I bark, starting to tuck Mara's things back into her purse. But my fingers pause on the last item. The envelope. Because the creamy paper, embossed with gold around the edges, has my name on it. Written in Mara's elegant, familiar curving handwriting.

What in the world?

Daniel's asking questions, something about the stage. I wave a hand. I don't care. "Charge whatever you need to the company account," I reply. "Make sure this is safe, next time, before you go testing something prematurely."

Overnight Wife   155

The rest of the crew nod, sobered by the disaster. But my mind is a million miles away from here. I need to get to Mara. I need to be with my wife, to make sure that she's all right, after everything that just happened.

And along the way... I need to find out what this letter is all about.

I march out of the auditorium, tearing into the envelope as I go. A little part of me feels bad about snooping. But it has my name on it, after all. She clearly intended to give it to me, before this whole mess happened, and interrupted whatever she'd had planned.

And with her in the hospital, I need any sort of connection to her I can reach for. Any way to reassure myself that what the paramedic said on his way out of the doors is true —that she's going to be fine. That my wife will be okay.

But whatever I expected when I tear into the envelope and read her neat handwriting on the custom card she made for me, it wasn't this.

John,

The night we met, I let loose for the first time in my life. The next morning, I thought I should regret it. I thought I'd made a mistake. But I didn't. Letting you into my life—letting you change my whole life—was the best accidental choice I ever made.

Now, I think we might have made another one. A similar one, one that will change everything... but which might just be the best accident we could have hoped for.

I know I told you I wasn't ready for children. And that's still true. I'm not ready. I don't know if I'll ever feel ready. But apparently the world had other plans for us. Because I'm pregnant, John. I'm carrying your child.

And, if you're up for it too... I'd like to keep it. I'd like to start a family with you.

As long as we both agree, we'll keep pursuing our careers too. We won't lose sight of ourselves. No matter what happens, this will make us stronger, John. Just like everything else we've already faced, together.

I love you.

Beneath it, she included a drawing. It's me, I can tell that from a glance, but it's a me I've never seen before. Looking at that drawing, at how she views me when I look at her, I see a whole new side of myself—because that's what she brings out in me. A man I didn't even know existed before I met her.

A better version of me.

And now... My heart leaps. A huge smile breaks out across my face. *She's pregnant. My wife is pregnant.* We're going to have a baby together.

But as soon as the news hits me, an alternate, terrifying thought occurs. Because I remember her injury, the stretcher. *What if something happened?* What if she's hurt worse than the paramedics thought? What if...?

I can't even allow myself to finish the thought. I refuse. Instead, I stuff the envelope back into Mara's purse with the rest of her things and practically sprint toward the parking lot. I need to get to the hospital. I need to make sure my wife and our baby—*our baby, oh my God, we're having a baby*—are safe. I need to protect my family. Because now, no matter what happens, they come first, always.

15

MARA

"Mara?"

The voice is far off, far away from me, somewhere floating in my subconscious. It's familiar, reassuring. But I don't need to worry. Not here, not where I am. I'm lying in a field of tall grass, on a picnic blanket, cradled in my favorite place in the world—against John's chest, with his arms around me, protective, secure. Beside us on the blanket, a smiling little ball of joy beams up at us, gurgling happily. *Our baby,* I know, without needing to be told. *That's our child, with us.*

We're a family. Whole and complete.

It's a beautiful dream. A happy one.

"Mara!"

So why is somebody interrupting it? I shift against John's chest and lean back to look up at him. His mouth moves, his lips forming words.

"Mara, can you hear me?"

It's John's voice I'm hearing, I realize, belatedly, somewhere in a distant part of my brain that's slowly clawing its way back to reality. Back to consciousness, and to a world I thought I'd checked out of for the time being. I shift my body, and groan at the feeling. I can feel bruises all over me. My whole left side flares with pain, it's hard to move my left arm, and my head throbs like crazy, as if someone stuck the whole thing in a giant wood press, crushing my brain between two hard blocks.

"Mara, honey." John's voice sounds a little louder now, a little clearer. I roll toward him, moaning softly, and I feel his fingers twine through mine. Not the John of my dream, hazy and imagined, but the real one. Here, with me, beside me.

My eyelids flutter, and the bright white lights overhead spark a whole new rush of pain throughout my body. I groan again, louder this time, and I hear other voices now. Unfamiliar ones, male and female, murmuring something.

"—gaining consciousness, that's a good sign. Mrs. Walloway, can you hear me?"

My eyelids flutter again, and the hospital room swims into sudden, painfully intense focus. There's John, propped in a chair beside my bed, his hand wrapped around mine. My free hand is covered in bandages, attached to an IV. Something beeps somewhere over my head.

I blink, and another figure swims into view. A female doctor, flanked by two male interns, squinting at my chart. Before I can register anything else, John wraps his arms around me, crushing me to him.

"Thank God," he murmurs against my hair, kissing my cheek, my jawline, the corner of my mouth, until the doctor laughs softly.

"Mr. Walloway, please, let your wife breathe," she says.

But when he releases me, it feels harder to breathe than it was with his arms wrapped around me. Still, he doesn't let go of my hand, and I hold onto it for dear life as I blink

Overnight Wife

around the room, still trying to get my bearings. It comes back to me in flashes.

The ominous creak of that set piece overhead. Bianca's wide-eyed stare, her soft gasp. Me colliding with her, and then my head hitting the floor.

I don't remember anything after that.

"That was quite a knock to the head you took," the doctor is saying softly, and leans in to peer at my face. "Look at me, please."

I do, and am rewarded with a sudden sharp flash of pen light directly into my eyes. I groan in protest.

"Good dilation response," she murmurs, checking my other eye quickly, before she grips my chin and turns my head left and right. "Any pain, Mrs. Walloway?"

"Yeah," I groan, my voice coming out scratchy and thin. "I feel like my head is in a vice grip."

"Hmm. We'll give you another dose of Ibuprofen soon," she says. "What do you remember? Any gaps in your memory?"

"I remember pushing Bianca out of the way of the crash... then... I think I hit my head." I frown. "Did I pass out?"

The doctor nods. John looks furious suddenly, though not at me. It looks like he wants to punch something, though. Probably he's mad about the set collapse, or the negligence of whoever let that rope fray so badly before they hoisted up something so heavy on it.

I push the thought away. The doctor is talking again, and with an effort, I focus on what she's saying.

"I don't want to give you anything too strong, painkiller-wise, given your condition, but so far Ibuprofen seems like it should do the trick. You'll let me know, though, if you have any discomfort..."

Condition. My gaze drops from hers, toward my stomach. Oh God. John. He doesn't know yet. I glance at him, fear and worry warring in my mind. "John, there's something I need to tell you," I start, but he shushes me with a finger to my lips, leaning in to kiss my temple. It helps soothe the throb there, at least a little bit.

"I know," he murmurs. "I found your letter."

My heart leaps into my throat—and I know, because I can hear the sudden rise in beeping on the machine I'm attached to.

"I'll give you two a minute," the doctor says, wisely, and she ushers her two interns out of the room with a gesture. I wait until the door shuts behind them before I risk meeting John's gaze, not sure what I expect to see there.

What I find is sheer, pure joy. Unmistakable. Mingled with relief, as he touches my cheek, looks me over. "You're okay? Really?"

"I'm okay," I promise him, and he leans in to press his forehead against mine.

"When I found out... when I read that letter, and you were already in the ambulance on the way to the hospital... Mara, I can't tell you how worried I was. How much I feared losing you... and our child."

Our child. Two simple words. Two words that change everything. But his hand goes to my stomach, and when he caresses the flat plane of my belly, there's no sign of hesitation or regret on his face. Only excitement.

"It's really true? We're going to have a family."

I smile through a sudden sting of tears. Happy tears mixed with relief that my injury wasn't worse. "It's true," I tell him, and he kisses me again, slower this time.

My lips part beneath his, and I melt against him, sinking into that kiss, savoring his taste, the familiar part of his lips

Overnight Wife

against mine. It's crazy how just a few weeks ago, we didn't know one another at all, and now I can't imagine my life without him in it. I can't picture a future where we aren't together.

When we draw apart, I lean my head on his shoulder with a contented sigh, our fingers entwining. "I meant to tell you this news under better circumstances," I say, and I can feel the vibration in his chest as he laughs softly.

"It doesn't matter. All that matters is you're safe." He kisses the top of my head again, his arm tight around me.

The words strike a memory in me. Bianca's wide, fearful eyes, and her expression as I tackled her out of the way. I sit upright again, my brow furrowing. "What about Bianca? She was there too; was she hurt?"

John's expression darkens again, just like it did earlier. "Oh, Bianca is just fine. I wouldn't be too worried about her."

I frown. "What happened?"

He tells me everything, then. About the fray in the rope, the cut Bianca must have made before the crew hoisted the set piece into the air. About her sister, John's ex, and why she was trying to get back at him. "She claims she didn't want anyone to get hurt, that she just wanted to frighten you, but..."

I grimace. "She could have killed someone. She could have gotten injured herself, or the crew could have dropped that on their own heads." I ball my fists, but John brings his hand to rest over them.

"I fired her, of course," he says. "I'll press charges too, if you want."

There's a beat where I consider it. I think about how John could afford to ruin that girl's life. But then I shake my head. People like that are always the authors of their own worst miseries. And now she's jobless, too, and no doubt with a black mark on her resume. "It's enough to never have to see her again," I mutter, leaning back into John's side as his arm snakes back around me, his fingers tracing through my hair. "She really wasn't hurt, though?"

John shakes his head. "She was fine. Shaken up, that was all."

"Good." I heave a sigh. "Is that crazy? I should probably hate her, but I wouldn't want her to get injured. Even if it would have been her own stupid fault."

"That's not crazy." John kisses my temple. "You're a good person, Mara. Maybe too good sometimes." He smiles.

I roll my eyes. "Lea always tells me that too. Actually, I believe her exact words are that I'm 'sickeningly good.'"

"I'm inclined to agree." He grins and kisses me again, softer this time. "It's both the best thing about you, and probably your only flaw—that you can't just stick up for yourself and be an asshole when you need to." He winks. "But don't worry. I can handle that side of things for the both of us."

I laugh and roll my eyes, shoving his chest gently. "You can't be that big of an asshole, or you'd have already hauled that girl off to jail with six different restraining orders."

His expression darkens. "Believe me, I was tempted. Especially after seeing you injured... But I thought about you, and I figured you wouldn't want me to. Not before I talked to you about it."

"Well. I guess we balance each other's bad and good sides out pretty well, don't we?" I grin and reach up to cup his cheek.

"I love you, Mara," he whispers, not for the first time, but it feels new all over again, sends a chill down my back and makes my belly tighten with excitement.

Overnight Wife

"I love you too." I reach down to cup my belly. "And I hope you love our child just as much."

"Believe me." He kisses the tip of my nose. Then my cheek. My jawline. "I already do," he whispers, his breath hot against my skin as he kisses his way lower. Down the edges of my collarbone, across the hospital gown I'm wearing. Until his lips reach my belly. He gently kisses me, through the thin fabric of the gown, hard enough that I can feel the heat, the outline of his lips against the soft skin of my stomach. "I can't wait to start this family with you, Mara Walloway," he murmurs.

And with his lips pressed against my stomach, I realize I can't wait for it either.

EPILOGUE

Mara looks incredible in that gown. It's bright red, tight in all the right places. A cascade of glitter and silk. It flares in just the right place to hide the bump underneath.

Less than a month now, until the newest member of our family joins us. I can't wait to meet him—we opted to find out the sex in our last ultrasound. We're having a boy. My parents would have been thrilled, if I hadn't cut them out of my life for the time being.

It won't be forever. I'll let them see their grandchild someday. It's important to Mara that we rebuild a relationship with them at some point, too. After all, family is family. But for now, I'm strong-arming my parents until they behave and start to treat my wife with the respect she deserves.

No more gold-digging comments. No more implying she's some kind of kept woman, or anything less than the brilliant architect of the best reviewed play about to leave previews in this city.

Tonight is opening night. Everything we've worked toward. And even eight months pregnant, Mara looks like the most beautiful woman on the red carpet tonight. She blows all the actresses out of the water, without even trying.

And I'm the lucky man who got to show up on her arm.

"How does it feel to be married to LA's biggest startup heartthrob?" one of the reporters asks, and Mara catches my eye. I'm standing a little to the side of the red carpet, her purse tucked under my arm.

One glance is all it takes for me to read her mind, and I step in, bringing my hand to rest against the small of her back. "Shouldn't you be asking me that question?" I tell the reporter with a grin. It draws a laugh from the surrounding reporters. But it does the trick, too. I watch them jot down a note, and the next person to address Mara does it properly.

"What were some of your biggest challenges in creating this set?" they ask her.

Mara flashes me a grateful wink, and turns to answer for herself, talking enthusiastically about the design, the props, everything that went into giving this play the background life it needed.

There's already been buzz about the sets. Talk of award nominations. I wouldn't be surprised if Mara wound up with awards on her first attempt out in this business. After all, it's just the kind of perfectionist she is.

Just the kind of career-focused woman I married.

The reporters ask me a few questions as well, and I give my usual talk about Pitfire, about our goals as a company, and how this play ties into them. Toward the end, unprompted, I add a little about how it's been working with my wife—about how she inspires me to push myself, to question my decisions, and to always improve on old ideas. To never settle for the easy way, the way everyone expects you to take.

The reporters lap that up like kittens with spilled milk.

Overnight Wife

I'm usually not one to give interviews about my personal life or to talk about my dates with the general public. But this is different.

Mara isn't some date I've got on my arm for the time being. She's my wife. She's my forever. And I'll always be happy to tell the world how much better she makes my life and our work together.

When we finish with the press gauntlet, we're finally allowed into the theater. Mara loops her arm through mine, and I tug her close to my side, one hand slipping around her waist, then lower, unable to resist, tracing the familiar curves of her ass. She shivers against me, and shoots me a little half-annoyed, half-turned on glare. One I've gotten used to over the last eight months together.

"You are terrible," she whispers, but she's grinning as she says it.

"So that's a yes, you will meet me in the bathroom in fifteen minutes?" I whisper back, one eyebrow arched, a grin fixed on my mouth.

She rolls her eyes. "You don't want to even watch the play that we just spent months preparing?"

"We've seen the dress rehearsals approximately a hundred times," I point out.

"But this is different. It's opening night."

"Which means the actors will all be nervous, and it will, frankly, be worse than the first rehearsal," I fire back, and she laughs, but rolls her eyes in that way that tells me she knows I'm right. Even if she doesn't want to admit it.

I expect her to resist, but her lips purse, and she studies the balconies. Then, to my surprise, she shoots me a sly smile. "I have a better idea."

It doesn't take us long to give the reporters the slip. After all, they aren't allowed past the main lobby—except for the ones who have tickets in the orchestra section, down on the first floor. Mara and I climb up to the top together, and she slips a key out of her pocket. The key to the rear projector room—one with glass windows, and a view of the stage. But we put the sound board for this show one level down. The only things in this room are spare parts, extra bulbs for the huge spotlights... And a nice view of the stage, with our own private lock and key.

"Good thinking," I murmur, grinning as she pushes the door open. I don't wait, but drag her through it, one arm around her waist, and pin her against the windows, my lips going to her neck, tracing down the line of her dress toward her cleavage. "I knew I married you for your brains."

"I thought you married me because I was the sexiest bad dancer you ever met," she counters, wriggling her hips against mine to demonstrate. Between the bulge of her belly and the sexy shimmer of those hips, it's enough to drive me wild. I trace my hands over her stomach, following the wide curve over and down, until my hand slides between her thighs to cup her pussy.

She gasps a little, shifting against me as her desire builds.

"That too," I reply, grinning. "And for how fucking sexy you look in this dress... do you know how hard it's been to keep my hands off of you tonight?" I murmur, my hands sliding around to grip her ass, pulling her against me quickly.

She can already feel the hard bulge in my suit pants, I'm sure. I've been hard as a rock since the moment we stepped into this enclosed space. "Probably as hard as it's been to stop myself from getting too wet," she replies, shimmying against me. "After all, I'm not wearing any panties under this thing..."

Overnight Wife

"I also married you for your dirty mind, you know." I smirk.

"Dirty, or practical?" She arches an eyebrow with a grin, as down below us, the house lights dim, and the stage begins to brighten. "At least from here we have a view."

Gently, I turn her around so she's facing the window too. And then I draw her dress up, inching it higher and higher, my hands tracing along the hem as I do, fingertips trailing up the back of her thighs until I reach the crease where they meet her hips. I run my hands over her firm, tight ass, squeezing hard, drawing her back against me, grinding my hips against hers, before I dip one hand between her thighs.

She wasn't lying. No panties whatsoever. And clearly the wet factor really was becoming a problem. I stroke a finger along her soaking wet slit, coating my fingertip in her juices, swirling it against her entrance.

"My wife really is impressively dirty," I murmur against the back of her neck, my lips moving against her skin.

She shivers and arches her back against me. "My husband sure knows how to tease and toy with me," she replies, her breath so hot it fogs the glass she's leaning against.

Down below, the curtains part to reveal the stage she worked so hard on. The play that's a culmination of my long dream.

Our dream, now. Like everything else in our life, we share it. And we work best together. United.

"You are incredibly talented, you know that, Mara?" I nod toward the stage. "Look at what you built."

"What *we* built," she corrects softly, leaning back to kiss my cheek, even as I continue to stroke her slit faster, feeling her growing even wetter beneath my touch. "We did this together." Her hips arch beneath me, and I suck in a sharp breath as her ass grinds against my rock-hard cock.

"It's sexy, how well we work together," I reply.

In the foggy glass, I catch the reflection of her grin. "I couldn't agree more."

Below us, unaware, the play begins. The actors recite their lines—lines that, like I told Mara, the two of us have already heard at least a hundred times. But she's right, too. There's something different about tonight. About this being the real thing, the true first performance—even if there have already been reviewers sitting in on rehearsals for the bigger newspapers. Tonight is the night that will determine the play's real performance. How the LA theater crowd—and the world's bigger crowd on the whole —views it.

The anticipation and the adrenaline just make every-thing hotter, as I spread Mara's legs gently, my fingers pressing inside her, one at a time, until I have three deep in her pussy and she's breathing so hard half the glass is fog now.

"Fuck me, John," she gasps, and I grin.

"That's the idea." I kiss the back of her neck, draw a stray strand of her hair up out of the way. "But first, I want you to come for me, wife."

Her hips buck as she starts to rock against me. Her pussy still feels as tight as ever, but combined with the sight of her big, pregnant belly, it's hotter than ever to watch her. To know that I put that baby in her belly. That she's mine, as the ring glinting on her finger declares to the whole world.

Her head falls back against my chest and she lets out a long, moaning gasp as her first orgasm hits. I pin her against me, hold her body as she trembles, and keep moving my fingers inside her, loving the way her pussy contracts and

Overnight Wife　　171

releases around my fingers, grasping, convulsing with pleasure.

"God, you are fucking perfect," I whisper.

Then I undo my belt buckle, and push down my pants, bringing the head of my cock to rest against her soaking wet entrance. I swirl the tip back and forth along her slit, coating myself in her juices, teasing, until she's rocking back against me, one of her hands reaching back to grip the back of my neck, holding herself up.

"Fuck me, John," she begs. "Please, please fuck me."

I can never resist. Not when she asks me like that.

I push inside her, going slow, an inch at a time. Letting her feel every inch of my cock, and savoring the way her tight pussy clenches around me, her muscles tightening and relaxing as I go, each inch more delicious than the last. Finally, I'm buried all the way inside her, up to the hilt. For a moment, I don't move. I stay there, savoring the feel of her.

I'll never get tired of this. I can't imagine ever having enough of my sexy, gorgeous wife.

"You're mine," I whisper, my hands sliding around her hips. One resting along her hip bone, and the other cupping her belly.

"I'm yours," she agrees, tilting her head back until her lips find mine. "And this baby is yours."

"I put our baby inside you," I murmur. Her pussy tenses around me, her muscles clenching with the shiver that passes through her body at those words.

"Fuck yes you did," she breathes, in a way that makes me grin, undoes something in me.

I draw out of her, just a little, and drive back in, hard enough to draw a gasp from her lips. Then I shift my hips, doing it again, again. Before long, we find a rhythm, my cock driving into her, our hips colliding with each thrust.

Far below us, on the stage, the play goes on. The actors recite their lines. The stage hands move in the background, unseen, trained by Mara to do their jobs at the exact right times. To be the people behind the curtain, invisibly creating a fantasy world for the audience to lose themselves in.

Just like the world we're losing ourselves in here. Only the two of us, savoring the fruits of our labor, in every sense.

When she finally comes again, it makes her whole body shake, and her knees go weak. I have to pin her against me, holding her up until I finish, coming deep inside her with a guttural groan that draws an answering moan from her lips.

We wind up staying in the booth for the whole first act. Neither of us want to leave each other's sides. And my hands don't want to leave her body. It doesn't take long for us to get hot and bothered again, just by one another's proximity. I already know, as I pull her into my arms once more, kissing her until I can feel her heartbeat against my lips, pounding in her throat—I will never be able to get enough of her.

But that won't ever stop me trying.

By the time the lights come on at intermission, we're a mess, but neither of us care. She straightens her hair as best she can and draws me out of the booth, back into the noise and bright lights of the theater with a huge grin on her face.

"Who'd have thought?" she calls over her shoulder as we head toward the main part of the theater, catching claps and nods of approval the whole way as we go. "That blowing off steam in Las Vegas could turn into such a productive move for both our careers." She winks and I laugh, pulling her back to my side to steal another kiss from her.

"Not to mention a productive move for our whole lives." I bring my palm to rest against her belly. "It might have been

Overnight Wife   173

a crazy move for both of us, Mara, but I have to say... I chose the right woman to elope with that night."

She laughs and leans up to tweak my nose. "Hope you don't have any regrets lingering, because it's way too late to apply for that annulment."

"Believe me, Mara." I cup her cheek in my hand. "Marrying you is the best decision I've ever made."

She sinks into my kiss again, and just then, as we're pressed together, I feel it. A gentle little kick, as our son pushes between us. It makes us both laugh, and I bring my palms to rest against her belly. My parents might have been assholes to Mara, but they were right about one thing—family is everything.

And this little family, the three of us? They're the most important thing in my whole world.

Manufactured by Amazon.ca
Bolton, ON